"I don't re
the swamp."

Laura's gaze shifted to the side. "And even if I did, there's no reason to think that it could happen again."

Drew took a deep breath. And held out his hand.

She slipped her fingers in his and a prickle of electricity shot through him, skittering up his arms.

His breath caught, and he focused on the soft flutter at the base of her throat. He longed to taste its sweetness, to run his tongue along the graceful sweeping curve of her neck.

His mouth went dry.

He forced his gaze away. He couldn't be thinking like this. He needed to put her out of his mind and forget about her. Yet at the same time he felt a need to protect her. To take care of her.

But she was meant to die.

Books by Cynthia Cooke

Harlequin Nocturne

Rising Darkness #23
Black Magic Lover #96

CYNTHIA COOKE

Many years ago, Cynthia Cooke lived a quiet, idyllic life caring for her beautiful eighteen-month-old daughter. Then peace gave way to chaos with the birth of her boy/girl twins. Hip-deep in diapers and baby food and living in a world of sleep deprivation, she kept her sanity by reading romance novels and dreaming of someday writing one. With the help of Romance Writers of America and wonderfully supportive friends, she altered her life's path and fulfilled her dreams. Now, many moons later, Cynthia is an award-winning author who has published books with Harlequin, Silhouette and Steeple Hill. If you enjoy page-turners that keep you glued to your seat and reaching for the one you love, then pick up one of her books. But if you do, if you take a ride over the edge and into the dark, don't forget to *turn on the lights.*

BLACK MAGIC LOVER

CYNTHIA COOKE

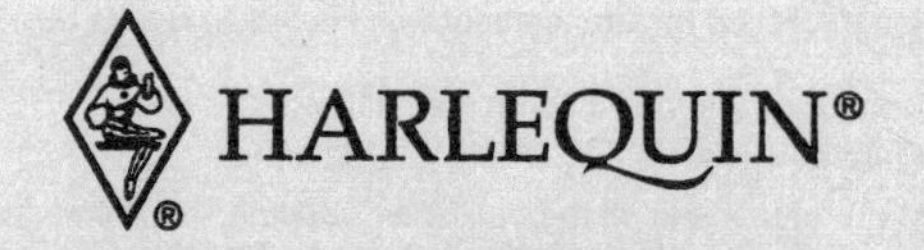

TORONTO • NEW YORK • LONDON
AMSTERDAM • PARIS • SYDNEY • HAMBURG
STOCKHOLM • ATHENS • TOKYO • MILAN • MADRID
PRAGUE • WARSAW • BUDAPEST • AUCKLAND

ISBN-13: 978-0-373-61843-9

BLACK MAGIC LOVER

This edition published by arrangement with Harlequin Books S.A.

For questions and comments about the quality of this book please contact us at Customer_eCare@Harlequin.ca.

www.eHarlequin.com

Printed in U.S.A.

Dear Reader,

Turn the first page and step into a world rich with the mystical. What looks like a quaint Louisiana bayou town filled with simple good folk is anything but simple. Turn on the light and hold your breath as Drew Michel fights against a powerful voodoo ritual that has targeted the woman he loves—the woman he would die to protect.

In *Black Magic Lover,* something dark and wicked is going on in the bayou. What looks like a small-town birthday bash is actually much more sinister and deadly—a voodoo ritual meant to appease the spirits and bring forth a demon to protect the town's citizens and help them prosper. And what it wants in return is a sacrifice.

Can Drew fight the townspeople? Can he prevail over a demon or will he succumb to the power of black magic and lose it all?

This story is about love triumphing over evil, because in the end as we fight our day-to-day battles, the only thing that matters, the only thing worth fighting for is love.

Thanks for taking this ride with me! Enjoy, and don't forget to *turn on the lights.*

Cynthia

Please visit my Web site at www.cynthiacooke.com.

To my family—I love you.

Chapter 1

Hurry back to Lionsheart before it's too late! Your mother never left the bayou.

Tendrils of anxiety squeezed Laura Larame as she recalled the whispered phone call that caused her to return to the Louisiana backwoods. She hadn't seen or heard from her mother in twenty years. It had been so long, she could hardly remember what she'd looked like, and yet, every now and then, her mother's voice would echo in the back of Laura's mind, haunting her.

Reminding her of all she'd lost.

Laura sat in the backseat of the cab, barely noticing as cityscape gave way to countryside, which gave way to bleak isolation. For days she'd tried to ignore the cryptic call, tried to focus on her work at the firm, but she couldn't stop wondering, was it true? Was it possible that her mother was alive and well, and living down here in this…swamp?

Laura's boss gave her the leave of absence she'd requested, and her roommate gave her the push she'd needed. *Find out what happened to your mother. Go after what you want, girl. Take control of your life. Take charge.*

Babs had been right. Laura had let life kick her around long enough. It was time she took a chance. Even if it was only on a half-baked hope that her mother was alive and living right here. She needed to explain how she could have abandoned Laura.

"Are you sure you want to go all the way to Lionsheart?" the cab driver asked. Dark, wary eyes set deep under salt-and-pepper eyebrows watched her through the rearview mirror.

"Yes," Laura answered, her voice unwavering. Her gaze dropped to a plastic statue of the Virgin Mary hanging from the rearview mirror, swinging back and forth. Back and forth.

"How 'bout I drop you at Larame Manor? People… people who wander too deep into the Atchafalaya Swamp…sometimes they don't come back."

A chill swept through Laura. The cab driver couldn't have known how dead-on he was. But she'd made it out…once.

The cab slowed in front of the large white home

with massive Doric columns and a pristine lawn, *Larame Manor.* The home of her stepgrandparents and the main house on a two-hundred-acre estate that encompassed the bayou and Lionsheart—the last place she'd lived with her mother.

The Larames were the closest relatives she had, even if they weren't blood. Their only son, Paul, had adopted her after he had married her mother, and from what Laura could gather, they were the ones who paid for her years at the boarding school. And yet she'd never heard from them. Not once.

An old familiar ache replayed like a worn-out sad song—the longing for family. For her mother. Resentment caused her to seethe inwardly. She would not partake in a pityfest today. And she wouldn't push herself onto unsuspecting relatives who never wanted any claim on her in the first place. All she wanted was answers, and she wanted those from her mother.

"Please continue to Lionsheart," she said.

He stiffened and they drove across a narrow bridge above the black, murky swamp.

"Devil's Walk, they call this bridge," the cab driver said, his voice barely above a whisper.

Laura stared into the water and felt anxiety rising within her, tightening her chest. She searched the shadows creeping across the water's surface looking for… She didn't know what. It was there, hidden in the dark depths of her mind, but she couldn't quite grasp it. A briny taste coated her tongue. She tried to swallow, but her throat closed. Her stomach twisted.

"Terrible accident happened right here," the driver said. "Things 'round here haven't been the same since."

They reached the edge of the bridge and Laura gasped, a long-lost memory forming, but then fading out, and leaving a raspy burning in her throat. She stared back at the black water. She'd gone into the swamp before. She knew what that murky water felt like against her skin, what it tasted like in her mouth.

A shudder coursed through her.

Before she could ask about the accident, she pitched forward as the cab came to a sudden halt on the other side of the bridge. The driver jumped out of the car, popped open the trunk and tossed her bag to the side of the dirt road.

Stunned, Laura quickly got out of the car. "What are you doing?"

The driver slammed the trunk shut. "This is as far as I go."

"Why? We're not there yet." She looked at the isolated swamp around her. "You can't leave me here." *Surely he wouldn't!* "I don't even know where Lionsheart is."

"I'm sorry. I won't go any farther. It's...dangerous." He demanded payment and glanced furtively around him.

Dangerous?

"Just continue straight down this road," he said. "You can't miss it."

Disbelief caught in Laura's throat. "What do you mean *dangerous?*"

"This part of the swamp is haunted…it's evil." He crossed himself over and over and muttered what sounded like a litany of Hail Marys. "Voodoo. Demons."

With a shaky hand, Laura fumbled in her wallet and handed him the fare.

"Are you sure you won't come back with me?" His dark eyes pleaded with her.

Demons? She looked around and a fresh wave of anxiety crashed over her. But she couldn't stop now. Not when she was so close.

"Yes. I'm sure."

Incredulity filled his face. Shaking his head, he climbed back behind the wheel and threw the car into a wild U-turn, spewing gravel and dirt all over her nice leather shoes. She jumped back.

"Superstitious idiot," she muttered.

She picked up the handle of her fallen suitcase and started pulling it down the road. The wheels, meant for smooth airport floors, bumped along, jerking her arm. This was crazy, she thought, and grimaced as black clouds thickened above her.

With each step, the swamp grew darker. Large insects droned around her head. A fine mist gathered and swirled above the water. Sounds echoed and carried through the air. Some she could identify—frogs, giant bees, birds—others she couldn't. A thin sheen of nervousness shrouded her.

For the hundredth time since she'd received the call, she racked her brain, trying to remember everything she could about Lionsheart, but only came up with jumbled images, and a knot of fear in the pit of her stomach. What if the house was dilapidated? What if no one was there? Questions cycled through her mind; doubts tore at her.

People say you can never go home. As she stared at the moss-drenched cypress trees reflecting off the black waters of the swamp and the thick tangle of green, Laura felt as if she had come home. And with that feeling came the overwhelming urge to turn and run.

She couldn't. Not yet.

The road curved. She rounded the bend. The house came into view. She stopped and dropped her bag. In boarding school, she'd wake up in the middle of the night, breathless and terrified, dreaming of this house. She had never been sure if it was real....

Until now.

With her heart lodged in her throat, she peered up at the house. The white structure soared three stories tall. Balconies adorned with swirling patterns of ironwork stretched across the front of each floor. Thick, green thorny vines were wrapped around tall columns, reaching skyward to smother the house and pull at the walls.

Laura stifled a shiver and again fought the instinct to flee. Nothing about this house was welcoming. Nothing moved. Both the grounds with their dark moldy fountains and the house seemed as quiet and still as a graveyard.

Then she scolded herself. She could do this. She had to do this. She hadn't been able to remember what had happened to her or her mother when they lived in this house, no matter how many different treatments the doctor had tried.

Now maybe she'd discover the truth.

Towing her suitcase, she filled her tight chest with a deep breath and cautiously climbed creaky steps onto the wide porch. With a trembling hand, she reached for the brass lion's head knocker on the front door, lifted it and let it drop. A loud thud reverberated around her, *through her.*

She scanned the large wooden door and expansive front porch. She'd spent her first eight years in this house. The answers she'd spent her whole life searching for were here. Someone must know what had happened and how she ended up alone in San Francisco.

Footsteps sounded within.

Laura stiffened and braced herself. The door swung open.

A tall man filled the doorway. Magazine-perfect

with dark brown hair and smooth chiseled lines underlying his face and strong jaw. His tailored jacket hung snugly across wide shoulders. Dress slacks hugged his form, betraying long, muscular legs. A cream linen shirt lay across smooth bronzed skin.

He was so unexpected, so out of place in the dank bayou, that for a long moment, Laura couldn't speak.

"Yes?" he said, his voice low and deep.

"I'm...um..."

His intense moss-green eyes, the same deep green hue of the swamp, locked onto hers. Questioning.

Say something. She blinked, moving her focus to his wide, generous mouth. She took a deep breath. "I—I'm looking for Delilah Larame."

The man stepped onto the porch, pulling the door shut behind him. He moved closer to her, stealing the air around her, or at least her ability to breathe it.

She took a quick step back, tripped on her suitcase and grasped for the rail. He grabbed her arm, steadying her with his strong grip. She felt his touch clear through to her insides.

"Who are you?" he asked, the deep tone of his voice making her heart beat double time.

What was with her? She was acting as if she'd never seen a man before. He reached forward, his fingertips almost grazing her cheek as he released a strand of her hair caught in a vine. For a heart-stopping moment, he held it then let it slide slowly through his fingers.

"Laura Larame," she answered, the words catching in her throat.

An unsettling hint of recognition filled his eyes as his gaze moved in a slow perusal of her face, her body…before finally settling on her dusty bag.

"My cab driver abandoned me back by the bridge." Story of her life, she thought as her tongue tripped, impairing her speech.

His perfectly sculpted dark eyebrows lifted in momentary surprise, before he nodded with understanding. "The locals can be a little superstitious."

"I gathered that," she said dryly.

For a moment neither of them spoke.

"I'm Drew Michel," he said then stepped back and opened the door. "Please, come in."

Drew. She knew that name; she just couldn't quite place it. She followed him, stepping through the front door and onto large black-and-white checkered tiles.

"I'm looking for my mother. Is she here?" Laura asked again.

His eyebrows arched with surprise. "Were you expecting her to be?"

"Yes," she said, feeling a touch confused.

"Why?"

Behind her, the front door closed with a resounding thud. She jumped, then turned and stared at a long staircase that stretched up into the shadows. Unfocused memories teased the back of her mind. Apprehension circled the base of her spine.

"I've received word that she's here," she muttered.

"Come into the living room," he said, his voice low and quiet, his words hanging between them in the gloom. "So we can talk."

Something lingering in the depths of his eyes sent warning bells ringing in her mind. She should leave. "I'm sorry. Maybe this wasn't such a good idea." She stepped back toward the door. "If my mother's not here—"

"Wait."

Was that a plea in his voice? She searched his face for the truth but couldn't find it.

He stepped close, too close. "It's been such a long time, Laura."

She swallowed. Something about the way he said her name, about the way his mouth moved over the letters, rolling them off his tongue and tasting them, knocked her off balance.

He reached out and traced his fingers along her jaw. She felt frozen, as if he'd trapped her under some voodoo spell known only to Louisiana natives—the rabbit caught in the eyes of the snake.

"There's something you should see." He turned and

walked toward a wide set of double doors, opening both at one time.

She shook off the stupor induced by his touch and followed him. Curiosity rising above her apprehension, she peered into the darkened living room and saw a fireplace centered on a far wall. Floor-to-ceiling windows covered with heavy green draperies flanked either side. A crystal chandelier hung above worn velvet furniture. Nothing here looked the slightest bit sinister or even familiar, just old and musty.

Slowly, she entered. Standing next to the window, Drew pulled open the drapes. Light flooded the room, highlighting a woman's portrait hanging above the mantel. Time stopped, as if the world spinning on its axis had come to a screeching halt and all that moved was the sudden thunder of Laura's heartbeat pounding in her ears.

From the portrait, her mother's image stared back at her, reaching deep into her heart and seizing it within a tight, painful grasp. Tears burned behind her eyes. She remembered this painting, and yet, she hadn't realized until this moment how much she looked like her mother.

"The resemblance..." she whispered then couldn't continue. The artist's deft strokes brought her mother's large pale blue eyes to life. Laura stared into them and felt almost as if her mother were sitting there looking back at her, peering deep into her soul.

Laura's knees weakened and a tight ball of need formed in the pit of her stomach. "Please, do you know where she is?"

"Delilah?"

"Yes."

He stood next to her, his warm breath caressing her cheek. "No, *chère*. She's *âme perdue,* a lost soul." His hypnotic voice washed over her, stealing the last of her energy. "You can see it in the depths of her eyes."

Laura was so tired and so afraid she'd reached a dead end. "I need to find my mother."

"We haven't seen her in years. Except in this portrait."

Her mouth opened on a soft breath. She looked up at him, on the brink of desperation and ready to plead for help. "I came so far, hoped so much. She has to be—"

China crashed, splintering across the floor.

Laura flinched. A woman stood in the doorway, her eyes wide with shock, her mouth open—a dark gaping hole in the center of her pale, white face.

"Delilah," she said, her voice an anguished cry.

"No, *Mère,* it's Laura."

The woman's gaze moved quickly from Laura's face to the portrait then back to Laura again.

"Laura's come home," he added.

Home. The word echoed through Laura's mind and

mocked her. This wasn't her home. She didn't belong here. She looked up at her mother's portrait—a mirror image of herself.

A lost soul.

Chapter 2

"Oh, Laura, of course," the woman said and stooped to pick up the broken shards of porcelain.

Laura stared at her. Had the world suddenly gone mad? This woman said her name as if she knew her, as if she had been expected, as if she'd never left.

Drew touched her arm, and a rush of awareness pulsed through her. This was all too much. Her nerves were on overload.

"Laura, do you remember my mother, Martha Michel? She lives here and watches over the place like she did when we were small."

When *they* were small? Pieces snapped into place. She recalled a boy a couple years older than herself. "Drew," she whispered. *Miss Martha's son.*

She looked at his mother with her deep red lips and dark coiffed hair. Her features had the glamorous look of Hollywood starlets from a bygone era.

"You're Miss Martha," she said softly. A memory tickled the corner of her mind. "I remember your banana cookies with maple frosting."

A small smile softened the harsh lines of Martha's face. "Yes, I used to bake them for you all the time."

Another memory came rushing back. Drew twirling her about under the massive trees, spinning her around, until overcome with dizziness, they'd both fallen to the ground.

If she tried hard enough, she could almost remember his laugh. But something got in the way. A shadow in her mind that turned the laugh into something different, something she couldn't quite recall.

"Well, Laura, you certainly have grown up. You're the spittin' image of your mama," Martha said as she fussed with the broken dishes. "You must stay with us so we can catch up. Your mother's room—"

"My mother's room?"

"I've kept it just how it was when she left, waiting for her to return."

"Waiting?" Unbidden hope expanded within Laura. "Have you heard from her, then? Do you know where she is?"

"Isn't she with you?" Miss Martha's forehead

wrinkled in puzzlement. "We haven't seen or heard from Delilah in ages."

Laura's stomach dropped. "No."

"No worries. Like you, she'll be back some day. She has to come back. Paul left her this house."

Confusion washed over Laura and spun her around as easily as Drew had done when they were children.

Martha's tone dropped, becoming hushed. "Change is riding on the wind. I can feel it in my bones."

Laura looked up at Drew. "What is she talking about?"

"Lionsheart belongs to your mother," Drew explained. "This is why it would be appropriate for you to stay."

"I've been waiting a long time for you and your mother to return," Martha added, then walked into the foyer and toward the staircase.

"Then why hasn't anyone contacted me? Why the silence all these years?" Laura called after her, but Martha didn't turn back or respond.

"Be careful. They won't want you here. They won't want you to know." The hushed words spoken across the phone lines echoed through Laura's mind.

She cast Drew a questioning look. He stared at her, his expression unreadable. Then he hiked up a brow and gestured for her to follow his mother into the foyer.

But Laura wasn't sure she wanted to stay. Something about this house, about the two of them, scared her. Drew was incredibly good-looking, yet he had a tightness in his jaw, a turn to his lips that could almost be cruel.

She walked into the foyer, but stopped in front of the grand staircase and rested her hand on the scrollwork of the iron balustrade. She gazed up. Each step loomed before her. She glanced over her shoulder at the front door. Something warned her to walk out that door and never look back.

And never know the truth?

She chewed on her bottom lip.

Miss Martha stood on the landing at the top of the stairs and looked down at her, her gaze cool and dark. Her red lips lifted at the corners forming a small smile that for some reason didn't look quite right on her face. "Come on, Laura. I'll show you to your room."

Laura hesitated as an odd sense of dread rooted her to the floor. She was afraid to go up the stairs, afraid of what she'd find at the top.

Drew stepped next to her at the foot of the staircase. "*Mère,* perhaps Laura would be more comfortable staying at the Inn in town."

At once thankful and yet unexpectedly suspicious, Laura studied his face. Was there a reason he didn't want her to stay here? Something he didn't want her to see?

"Don't be ridiculous, Drew. We have plenty of

room here." Miss Martha's tone was sharp and left no room for debate.

Drew sighed and gestured for Laura to precede him.

She wasn't sure if she was relieved or not, but if she was going to find out what happened to her mother, she'd have a much better chance if she stayed right here, where she and her mother had once lived, rather than in town.

One by one, she forced herself to climb the stairs, her stomach fluttering with each creaking step. She could do this. It was just an old house, nothing more and certainly nothing to be afraid of.

So why the butterflies?

She stepped onto the landing and took a deep breath to settle her nerves. She'd almost succeeded until she saw her mother's photos lining the red-carpeted hallway. In a cool rush, chills tumbled down her spine.

She remembered this hall, remembered those pictures! There was so much she couldn't recall from her childhood days here. Selective amnesia caused by a terrible trauma, the doctor had told her. But she remembered these photos, remembered her mother taking them—a large spider spinning an intricate web, two eyes and a reptilian snout peaking above the shimmering surface of dark water, the deep incandescent pink of a blossom. There was even one of Laura as a child, black hair glistening, her gaze in an intent examination of a ladybug perched on her fingertip.

Soft, tinkling laughter echoed through her mind.

She examined closely the photo of herself. The way her hair shone in the sunlight, the small golden unicorn necklace that had been her favorite. It was working! Being in the house seemed to be pushing at the walls in her mind, opening cracks to her elusive past.

She continued down the hall, studying each photo. She stopped in front of one of her and Drew dancing beneath the spray of a sprinkler on a hot summer day. He'd been at that awkward adolescent stage, but she could easily see the man he would become in his features as a boy. How could she not have recognized him the moment she'd laid eyes on him?

She turned to him as he stood slightly behind her. "I've forgotten so much."

"Now that you're back, you'll probably remember a lot more. The sights, sounds, all of this," he said, gesturing with opened arms, "will stimulate your memories."

"I hope so. In San Francisco no one knew anything about my past. There was no one to help me keep what few memories I had alive. After a while, I was no longer sure what was real or what I'd imagined."

His green eyes softened. "That must have been tough."

"The worst part was forgetting so much about my mother. And not knowing what happened to her."

Not for the first time since she received that phone call, sadness seeped through her. She would reconnect with her past; she would remember what happened to her mother. Even if that meant she had to stay here in this house.

"Come, your mother's room is at the end of the hall," Miss Martha said, and continued forward.

Her mother's room.

Laura followed, curiosity growing within her. But as the door loomed in front of her, a tight band of anxiety squeezed her chest, smothering the lingering excitement she'd felt from viewing her mother's photos.

Slowing, she looked back at Drew. He was still standing by the pictures, although he no longer looked at them. Instead, he looked past her toward his mother, his expression pinched with dread.

What was wrong?

Laura followed his eyes to her mother's door. Miss Martha's sharp gaze pinned Laura in place. An image flickered through her mind just out of reach, something dark, something bad. Laura's heartbeat thumped. Her palms dampened.

She stopped.

A wave of dizziness surged through her. Pain pierced her temples. She reached up and pressed her fingertips against her skin. White blotches blurred the edge of her vision. Through squinted eyes, the hallway lengthened. Her mother's door stretched farther away from her.

What was happening?

Laura opened her mouth to speak, but no sound came out. She swayed, reaching. She heard Drew call her name, but his voice sounded faint as if coming from far away. Shadows flickered. The air thinned. She gasped, but couldn't draw a breath.

The floor tilted, walls shifted.

Blackness swallowed light.

She was falling, a silent scream trapped inside her throat.

"*Hush, baby,*" her mother's voice urged. "*Don't make a sound. We have to get you out of this house.*"

"Laura?" Drew's tone was insistent, demanding. "Laura!"

Laura's eyes fluttered open. Everything rushed back into focus. Drew's brilliant green eyes gazed into hers. His strong arms held her and, for a moment, she felt safe. For a whisper of a second, she remembered how it felt to have her small hands clutched in his. As she looked at him, she heard the distant sound of his laughter echoing in her mind.

But for some reason it made her want to cry.

Son of a bitch! Drew pulled Laura closer as the dead circled them, hovering, gesturing wildly, their mouths opening and closing in soundless shouts. Some were grotesque while others appeared benign, looking as they must have in life. How they chose to appear to him made no difference to Drew. He hated them all, hated that he had the curse that allowed him to see them.

Long ago he'd learned to tune them out, to make them disappear. In fact, they were the reason he'd left this mausoleum that had been his childhood home. He'd begged his mother and Uncle Randal to send him to boarding school, to send him anywhere, as long as it was away from there. Once he'd left, he hadn't wanted to return and had only done so once before.

Until now.

Drew hadn't seen a single shadowy specter since arriving earlier that day. He'd thought that he'd succeeded in blocking them out and that this house wouldn't have the same power over him as it had had when he'd been young. Obviously, he'd been wrong. The spirits were back with a vengeance, surrounding Laura and doing everything they could to stop her from continuing down the hall.

And they'd succeeded.

What do they want? Why Laura?

And what had they done to her?

Fear knotted within him. He'd never seen such a swarm of ghosts before. Worse, he'd never seen them have an affect on the living. Laura went down like a ton of bricks. Was she sensitive to them? Did she feel them?

Did she see them, too?

Laura's eyes fluttered open again. Drew sucked in a relieved breath as her eyes met his. Immediately, her face filled with fear. He tightened his arms, pulling her close, hoping she wasn't cursed as he was. Hoping she couldn't see them.

His mother hurried toward them.

"What happened?" Laura tried to sit up, but wobbled then fell back against him.

He held her and brushed the hair off her face, concerned by her gray pallor and the cold clammy feel of her skin. "You fainted. Are you all right?"

"Fainted?" Her brows drew together in confusion. "I've never fainted before." Her laugh was strained. "I guess I should have eaten more today. I was too nervous to stop for lunch after I landed, and they hadn't served anything on the plane."

He stood and helped her to her feet, but she seemed too shaky to stand on her own. "You should rest." And then you should get the hell out of Dodge, he thought as the spirits surrounded them.

He turned to his mother who stood next to them. "*Mère,* can you get Laura some tea and something to eat?"

"Of course. Right away," she answered, and rushed past them down the hall.

He lifted Laura. She was much lighter than he

expected and smelled baby soft, like sweetness and innocence.

"This really isn't necessary," she protested, but tightened her grip around his neck.

At first he tried to ignore how nice she felt pressed up against him, but then realized he would rather focus on her than the throng of spirits protesting their progression down the hall.

"I can't have women collapsing in front of me. It wreaks havoc with my self-image." He struggled to keep his tone light and his eyes locked on hers, otherwise he'd start shouting at the specters to get the hell out of here, to leave this woman alone.

He'd worked hard to keep his life free of the dead. His youth in this house had been a waking nightmare. After he'd left, he'd spent years perfecting his skills at blocking the spirits. He no longer heard their voices or saw their grisly forms materializing out of nowhere. But now, after just a couple of hours back in this wretched house, he was battling them all over again.

As if he'd never been gone.

He took a deep breath and tried to clear his mind. He focused on the sweet smell of Laura, on the weight of her in his arms, on the tickle of her hair against his skin.

She squirmed. "Wait, please! Set me down."

Stunned by the sharp tone of her voice, Drew

stopped just outside her mother, Delilah's, bedroom door. "What is it?"

"I can't go in there," she insisted, her voice small and tight. "Not yet."

He looked at the spirits who'd suddenly stopped their useless attempts to block his path. "Why not?"

"I don't know. I'm not sure. I just...can't."

What was it about this room that seemed to have such a powerful effect on her? He set her down, then took a step back. Whatever was going on here, it had to do with this house and the spirits that lived here. And he wanted no part of it.

"I'm sorry—" he started, then stopped. Over Laura's shoulder, Paul's ghost stood smiling at him, throwing Drew's old baseball up in the air and catching it. Up and down. Up and down. He looked just as he had twenty years ago when he'd been married to Laura's mother, when he and Drew used to play ball back when life was good, before the accident, before the ghosts, before Delilah disappeared and Laura almost died.

Was that why he was here now? Because of Laura?

The night of Paul's accident, Drew had awakened to find his cousin standing at the foot of his bed looking lost and confused, trying to say something but instead emitting an awful gurgling noise.

Blood seeped from a deep gash in his head and

ran down his face and neck to saturate the stiff white collar of his business shirt. Rheumy blue eyes set deep in concaved eye sockets stared out of bluish-white-tinged skin. Thin lips stretched back over yellowed teeth. The putrid stench rolling off him had filled Drew's nose, and he'd felt powerless with nowhere to run.

Paul had come back to him again and again, but he'd never looked as awful as he had that first night. Yet still he came, always trying to say something Drew couldn't understand.

Over the years, other spirits had come and gone, but none had bothered him as much as Paul.

Drew turned back to Laura. Her eyes were closed and she was inhaling deep, slow breaths. It was almost as if she could sense the spirits around her, trying to stop her. She shouldn't stay here. The spirits were drawn to her. He was afraid of what they might try to do.

At last she looked up at him.

"Better?" he asked.

She nodded and gave him an apologetic smile that tempted him to pull her back into his arms. She was an enigma that he couldn't wrap his mind around. One minute he wanted to get as far away from her as possible and in the next, that hint of sadness and vulnerability made him want to reach out and hold her.

To protect her.

Which was totally ridiculous.

He didn't protect people. He didn't get involved. He stayed on the sidelines, isolated in his house outside Atlanta. He didn't form attachments or relationships. He put all his energy into his work and was more successful because of it. With a curse like his, life was a whole lot easier that way.

He led Laura toward the room next to his instead, his hand lingering on her waist as he gestured for her to precede him. He hesitated in the doorway, staring at her. She'd grown into such a beautiful woman with her long, silky black hair and pale blue eyes.

"How's this room?" he asked.

She nodded, lush lips curving into a tentative smile. He couldn't help wondering if they were as soft as they looked, and if they tasted as sweet.

Merde, what was he thinking?

Without saying a word, he crossed the room to the French doors and opened them. He stepped out onto the bedroom's small balcony that overlooked the swamp and closed his eyes as a slight breeze washed over him.

When they were small, it had been his job to look after her. That must be why he couldn't make himself turn around and walk out the door now. Why he was so drawn to her. He gazed out at the bayou, at the sunlight glistening on the water. So beautiful.

So deadly.

They'd both almost died that night in the swamp.

That was the last time he'd seen her, but not the last time she'd been in his thoughts.

A soft footfall revealed her presence behind him.

Out of nowhere, pain arced across his eyebrows. He dipped his head as the metallic smell of blood filled his nose. He knew what was coming, although it had been a long time since the last one had hit him, the preludes to his visions were always the same.

He pinched the bridge of his nose and closed his eyes, imagining himself bathed in an intense bright light. Hoping the light would keep the dark at bay.

But the smell wouldn't go away.

His heartbeat thudded in his temples. Panic shot straight through him. Water sloshed forming a puddle on the balcony floor. He stared down at it, watching it grow. He took a deep breath. "White light, white light, white light," he chanted under his breath.

"Did you say something?" Laura asked, her voice sounding melodic as she stepped closer to him.

He cringed, moving away from her, the balcony pushing sharply into his gut. He grasped hold of the railing with whitened knuckles. Water droplets fell on the back of his hand. He stared at the drops, watching them pool and run off his skin.

Out of the corner of his eye, he caught sight of long black hair dripping swamp water, and squeezed shut his eyes.

"Rest. You should rest," he muttered through clenched teeth.

"I'm fine." She touched his arm lightly, barely a touch at all, and yet, a bone-deep chill seeped through him.

This bloody curse.

Seeing ghosts wasn't bad enough. No, he had to have the visions, too. He had to see those touched by death. He turned back toward the room, stepping through the widening puddle at his feet. He managed to keep Laura in his peripheral vision, and still avoid looking directly at her. He was afraid of what he'd see, afraid of what she'd already become.

His stomach lurched and nausea churned his insides. It had been years since this had happened to him. He thought he'd beaten the visions, thought he was free of them. Why here? Why now?

Why her?

He walked past her into the room. "After you rest, I'll drive you into town and help get you settled in the Inn. This house is old and moldy, it would be better for you to stay in town."

"Won't you be here?" she asked.

"Only for a couple of days," he answered, while still avoiding looking at her.

"Oh." Disappointment laced her voice.

His vision started to fold and bend. He hardened

his gaze and straightened his spine as he tried to stave off the inevitable.

"Drew," she said, softly, touching him once more.

He hesitated, not wanting to, but not able to stop himself, either. He turned toward her. He had to see.

Merde. It took everything he had to keep his expression impassive, to keep the air from whooshing out of his chest, the cry from escaping his lips.

This was why the spirits had been circling. His gaze traveled the length of her hair, water-soaked and tangled with duckweed and hanging in wet ringlets across her shoulders. Her yellowed skin was sallow and looked even paler beneath the dark smudges ringing her wide, blue eyes. A gaping hole oozed red from her shoulder—a bullet wound.

Death's touch clearly placed.

His visions of death hadn't come often, surely not as often as the spirits themselves. But they had always sickened him, making him feel exactly what he was—powerless. And from the extent of death's touch in this vision, he'd say Laura only had a couple days before death claimed her.

Damn this curse! Why did he have to know if there wasn't anything he could do about it? And why Laura? Hadn't she been through enough? Anger and frustration surged within him, and yet there wasn't anything he could do to stop what was to come. He couldn't yell, kick the bed, put his fist through the wall. No, he had to stand there and pretend he didn't know Laura was about to die.

Defeated, he sat on the side of the bed and dropped his head into his hands. At one time, he'd actually thought he could save death's victims. Walking corpses, he used to call them. He thought if he could figure out why death had touched them, he could change their fate, alter destiny. But he had been young and optimistic. Now he knew death couldn't be defeated, nor destiny changed. He'd traveled down this road too many times before. It only went one way.

The mattress sank as she sat next to him. Reluctantly, he lifted his head and looked at her.

"Drew, I have to believe my mother must have gotten into some kind of trouble to keep her from coming for me. If I could just stay in this house for a little while, I'm sure I'll be able to remember, or at least figure out what happened to her."

She said the words completely unaware she carried death's tragic touch, that she spoke through blue-black lips, cracked and swollen. He turned away again, unable to continue watching, his heart sinking with the knowledge that she didn't have long to live.

He cleared his throat, trying not to betray the distress echoing through him. "What makes you so sure?"

"I don't know." The sadness in her voice plucked

at his heart, but it didn't matter now. There wasn't anything he could do to help her.

She touched his hand. Torment twisted through him.

"Drew, how much do you remember from when we were children?"

Swamp water leaked from her mouth and ran down her chin.

"Can you tell me? Help me to remember?"

He remembered pulling her out of the swamp. She'd almost died, would have died, if he hadn't saved her. How was he going to stand by and watch her be taken from him all over again? Only this time for good.

"I remember a lot of things," he said.

"What can you tell me? Specifically? I know if I could remember more, it would help me find my mother." Her voice cracked with emotion.

Maybe if he could just persuade her to go home, to get away from the swamp, then she'd be okay. One thing was certain: if she stayed here, she would die.

He turned back to her. She looked normal again—her skin flushed pink and beautiful, her eyes bright and shining. For just a moment, his mind raced as he tried to think of a way to save her, to stop death this time.

But then the futility of his wishes stole back in. There wasn't anything he could do for her. Soon she would join Paul and all the other troubled spirits who haunted these corridors.

Why had he been able to save her before, if the swamp was only going to claim her anyway?

"What brought you back to Lionsheart?" he asked, his voice tripping over the words. "Now, after all these years?"

Her gaze locked onto his, reaching deep inside him to grasp hold of his heart. "I believe my mother's here. I think she needs me."

"No one has seen your mother in years."

"So I've been told, but all that does is make my job harder. I can't leave until I discover the truth. I need to know why she didn't come back for me. I need to know whether she's dead or alive."

"What do you remember about the last night you were here?"

She bit her lip, her gaze moving to the floor.

"Do you remember anything?"

"No," she said, her voice a hoarse whisper. "I've tried, but I only get disjointed images.

"That last night you were here, the last time anyone saw you or your mother, you almost drowned in the swamp."

She swallowed, her eyes widening.

"Laura, you can't stay here. You need to go home before..."

"Before?" Her face paled.

"Before it happens again."

Chapter 3

"I don't remember almost drowning in the swamp," Laura said, her gaze shifting to the side. "And even if I did, there's no reason to think that it could happen again."

Seeing this was going nowhere, Drew took a deep breath. "I tell you what, let's go downstairs and get something to eat. We can continue this conversation after we've both had a chance to recharge." He forcibly relaxed and held out his hand.

She slipped her hand in his and a prickle of electricity skittered up his arms. Awareness, thick and hot, shot through him. His breath caught as his gaze fell on the flutter at the base of her throat. For a moment, he longed to taste its sweetness, to run his tongue along the graceful sweeping curve of her neck.

His mouth went dry, as his eyes fell lower.

Beneath the smooth cotton of her blouse, the gentle swell of her breasts rose with each breath she took. Soft. Inviting. He forced his gaze away. He couldn't be thinking like this. He needed to put her out of his mind and forget about her. And yet, at the same time he felt a need to protect her. To take care of her.

He saved her once, and he felt responsible for her now. That must be why her hand felt right in his. As if it was meant to be there, as if she was meant to be with him.

But she was meant to die.

"Is everything all right?" she asked, her wide blue eyes perusing his face.

He stiffened. "Yes."

He dropped her hand and stood, then waited for her to precede him out the door. He would have to be careful not to let himself want her. He couldn't help her. He couldn't fight death. He'd long ago given up on that fruitless endeavor. And to let himself think about her too much would be disastrous. He closed his eyes and hardened himself to the knowledge that very soon she'd be dead.

The sooner he put some distance between them the better.

The rich aroma of Andouille sausage frying in the pan filled the kitchen as they entered the room.

"Laura, how are you feeling," his mother asked as she quickly stirred the meat.

"Better," Laura answered.

Drew led her to the table, pulled out a chair for her and tried not to notice when her hair brushed against his skin.

"Smells great," he said, striving to think about the food and not Laura.

"I'm sure it's been a long time since you've had gumbo," his mother said, shaking salt and pepper into the stew.

"None that could compare to yours." It had been at least ten years since Drew had been home for a visit. He'd been too busy with law school and then working overtime to prove himself to the partners at the law firm. He'd built an impressive track record, becoming very successful, but that didn't leave a lot of time for a private life or long visits home to the swamp.

For a moment, guilt mingled with a touch of nostalgia filled him. But then, Paul appeared next to his mom and reminded him why he'd left home so early to begin with.

His cousin's ghost leaned over the pot as if he were inhaling the rich aroma of the gumbo simmering on the stove. He turned to Drew, his mouth curving into a wide, wicked grin.

Martha stiffened, but otherwise made no appearance that she was aware of him.

But she was.

Drew had long suspected that she had the curse, too, and though it wasn't something she'd ever talked about, Drew knew.

"Need any help?" he asked.

"No, it's all ready." She ladled three bowls full of gumbo and placed two of them in front of him and Laura on the table.

"I hope you didn't go to a lot of trouble," Laura said, and breathed deeply of the steam rising from the rich brown stew.

"No trouble. I've been cooking all day preparing for the party."

Laura looked up. "Party?"

His mother sliced up thick pieces of French bread and put them in the bowl on the center of the table. "Drew's turning thirty. A special time in a man's life. An awakening of his true nature. Around here, we celebrate that by throwing a big bash—an Awakening Party."

Drew choked on the spicy stew and beat a fist against his chest. He hated it when she did that. Sometimes she could be the sweetest woman, dripping with Southern charm, and then she'd get that far-off look in her eyes and say something truly creepy.

She quickly poured him a tall glass of sweetened iced tea from the pitcher on the counter. He sucked the tea down then handed the glass back to her.

"Thanks," he said as she refilled it then poured two more for herself and Laura.

"Anyway," she continued. "You'll have to come."

Laura leaned back in her chair. "No, I couldn't crash your party."

"If you're still here, you might as well come," Drew said, though hopefully by then he would be able to convince her to go home. He grabbed a piece of bread and tore off the crust to dip into his stew.

"Of course you'll come. Jeanne wouldn't have it any other way," his mother insisted and joined them at the table.

"Jeanne Larame? My stepgrandmother?"

"Yes, my sister-in-law. Do you remember her?"

Laura shook her head.

"She was Paul's mom. Your stepdad?"

Drew glanced around the room to see if Paul was still around, but thankfully he'd disappeared, again.

"I remember him." Laura's smile was thin and a touch sad.

"And I know Randal can't wait to see you, Drew," his mother said, turning to him. "He said something about talking shop."

Drew nodded, though he wasn't looking forward to the meeting. He knew what Randal wanted, what he'd always wanted—for Drew to come back home and work at the Larame law firm.

"I like Atlanta," he said. Even more, he liked how far away he was from this swamp.

"You live in Atlanta?" Laura asked, surprised.

"Yes, I just flew in today for a quick visit before the party. I arrived right before you did."

"Wow, what are the odds of us both coming back on the same day?"

She had a touch of sauce on the corner of her mouth. He fought an overwhelming urge to lean forward and kiss it away. She brushed her hair off her shoulders and bent over the bowl to take another bite.

"Do you remember gumbo?" he asked, unable to take his eyes off her.

She shook her head. "It's very good, though."

"So, where have you been all these years?" his mother asked Laura.

"San Francisco."

"And your mother wasn't with you?" She dunked a crusty piece of bread into her stew then looked up at Laura.

"No, I grew up in a boarding school. My mother… I haven't seen her in a long time." Laura stared intently at her bowl.

"That is odd," Martha said. "Delilah left quite unexpectedly, you know. After Paul's death none of us blamed her. We figured she wanted to start over somewhere else. But she didn't say where she was going. I certainly never imagined you weren't with her. I still find that very hard to believe."

"Really?" Laura asked, clearly surprised. "Why's that?"

His mother stood up to clear their bowls. "Because for Delilah, the sun rose and set on you."

Laura stared at her for a second, her eyes growing misty and filling with pain. Before Drew could ask if she was okay, she stood and stepped back from the table. "Thank you for dinner. If it's all right, I'd like to go upstairs and unpack."

Drew stiffened. He'd hoped he could have convinced her to leave before she got settled here.

"Sure. Take your time," Martha said.

Laura turned and left the room without giving Drew a second glance.

Paul was back, standing in the corner glaring at him as if he expected Drew to do something.

"The poor thing," Martha said, once Laura was out of earshot. "If Delilah was just going to abandon the girl like that, she should have left her here with us."

What was it Paul wanted from him? Why couldn't he just go wherever it was the dead are supposed to go and leave him alone?

"She would have ended up in a boarding school like I did, anyway," Drew said.

His mother sighed. "I suppose you're right. The

poor girl just seems so sad. Why don't you run upstairs and check on her?"

Drew took a deep breath and pushed back from the table. He wanted to check on her. He even wanted to be there for her and help her search for the truth about what happened to her mother, but he wouldn't. If he tried to comfort her, to tell her everything would be okay, he'd be lying.

Everything wasn't okay, and for her it never would be again. The only way to help Laura now would be to convince her to get as far away from this swamp as possible.

Tears burned in Laura's eyes, but she refused to let them fall. Hearing that her mother had actually loved her hit her harder than she'd expected. All the holidays and vacations she'd spent alone in the dorms waiting for a call, a visit from family, from a mother who hadn't come, forged holes of doubt in that love, holes so deep, they'd probably never be filled.

With her suitcase in tow, she stopped on the landing and focused on the door to her mother's room at the end of the hall. She wasn't sure why she was so afraid of that room, but knew it was the best place to start her search for answers. Determined, she headed down the hall. But with each step forward, her heart beat a little faster.

She racked her brain, pushing at the corners of her memories, trying to recall what the room looked like, smelled like. What could possibly be in there that scared her so much? Her stomach turned. Shadows shifted on the outskirts of her vision.

A feeling of being watched raised the hair on the back of her neck. She stopped and looked around, but saw no one. And yet, the sensation of a breath sliding down her back persisted.

She took another step forward.

"Laura," Drew called.

She turned and saw him step onto the landing at the top of the staircase.

He was looking past her again with that same pinched expression on his face that he'd worn earlier.

"Is everything all right?" she asked.

"Yes. I thought I'd check to see how you're doing," he said as he walked toward her down the hall.

"I'm fine. I was just..." She looked back toward her mother's room.

"How about we go for a walk?" he asked.

"Now?"

"Sure. Let's walk off our dinner." He took her hand in his.

The gesture surprised her and caught her off guard. How was it she felt so close to him, and yet, at the same time, felt as though she didn't know him at all?

Instead of going down the long drive from the direction she'd come, Drew took her along a path that curved around the back of the house and wound alongside the swamp.

"Where are we going?" she asked.

"To the graveyard."

A bird shrieked. A chill snaked along her spine. "What on earth for?"

"There's something I want to show you."

The path narrowed. Tall weeds encroached. A multitude of noises sounded around them—large insects or small animals scurrying about.

"Are you sure this is something I want to see?" She turned away from the grasses and looked out at the dark, still waters littered with cypresses standing tall on knobby roots.

Instead of answering, he picked up his pace.

"Drew!" She tripped on a rock, or at least she hoped it was a rock. Around here it could be anything. "Can we slow down here a minute?"

He stopped and turned back to her, the look in his eyes almost desperate.

"What's the matter?" she asked, suddenly afraid.

"I need to know why you've come back."

"I told you—"

"No. I mean why right now. Why today?"

Be careful. Not everyone will want you here. The warning rang through her mind. Could she trust him? She wasn't sure, but she wanted to. And worse, she could use his help to find her mother.

She should tell him.

"I got a call. I don't know why and I don't know who from. All the person said was that my mother never left the bayou. That I should come back quickly. And..." She looked him in the eyes, trying to gauge his reaction. "And not everyone will want me here."

He looked surprised and slightly disturbed. "Sounds cryptic."

She nodded. "Ominous, even."

"So you flew right down?"

"Took a leave of absence from my job and everything."

His mouth hardened. "Did you try calling here first? Talking to anyone to see if your mother was actually here?"

"Who would I call? I don't know anyone."

"Obviously someone knows you." His eyes narrowed to slits. "Someone who wanted to lure you down here."

Suddenly aware of how much bigger he was than her, and how much stronger, she looked around, searching for any sign that they weren't alone, but saw no one as the sun sank in the sky.

"Your mother isn't here and hasn't been here for a very long time."

Laura looked at the brackish water on one side of her and the tall grasses on the other, realizing there was nowhere to run. Why had he brought her there? What was he planning?

"Are you one of those people who don't want me here?" Her voice caught over her words, but she had to ask. Shadows lengthened, enveloping her.

He stepped close, kicking her heart into overdrive as his gaze locked onto hers. "I'm afraid for you."

Fear fluttered in her chest. "Why?" she asked, the word coming out in a strained whisper.

"The last time I saw you, you were floating right out there." He pointed to an area beyond them about fifty feet into the dark water. A thick tangle of vines choked the surface. How had she gotten out there? Was this what her mind had been blocking all these years?

"I swam out and saved you and almost drowned in the process. We were both taken to the hospital. By the time I was released, you were already gone."

Laura stared at the greenish-brown water and shivered. Deep inside, she felt the truth of his words.

"You didn't swim out there on your own that night, and whether you want to believe it or not, someone lied to bring you here now. You need to go back to the house, grab your bag and get out of here as quickly as possible."

His gaze hardened, scaring her even more than the darkening waters.

"And for your sake, I hope you never look back."

Laura didn't know what to say. She stared at the swamp, at the tangle of vines and, for a second, she could imagine them wrapping around her legs, her arms and pulling her under.

"Why would someone do that? I was just a little girl. And why would someone lure me back here to hurt me now? No one even knows me here."

"The reason doesn't matter."

Hearing the hard steel in his voice seemed reason enough, and yet she couldn't give in that easily. "Even if you're right I can't leave, not yet. I just got here. I haven't had the chance to talk to anyone yet, to find out anything about my mom. I need to know what happened to her."

He took a step closer to her. "I'll ask around for you while I'm here."

Yeah, right. Her back stiffened. "I have to stay."

He brushed past her quickly, heading back down the path toward the house, leaving her all alone in the darkening swamp.

Did someone really want to hurt her? Did *he* want to hurt her? Maybe she should go home. But if she were to leave, than that would mean she'd given up. She couldn't quit. Not after she'd come this far.

She walked back toward the house refusing to let Drew intimidate her. She wouldn't scare that easily.

She thought back to the whispered phone call and couldn't help wondering what the caller's game was. Where was her mother?

Be careful. Not everyone will want you here.

Chapter 4

Laura must have been more tired than she thought. After coming back to the house, she unpacked her bags then fell right to sleep. And from the stiffness in her back when she woke, she obviously hadn't moved much.

She got up, showered and dressed, then went downstairs to the kitchen to get a quick bite. She hoped Martha would give her a ride into town. She wanted to ask around about her mom before she ran into Drew again.

After a boiled egg and some toast, and with Miss Martha's keys in her hands, Laura stepped out the kitchen door. Unfortunately, Drew was leaning against a large tree staring out at the water. Waiting for her? She hoped not.

"I can take you into town," Drew said, turning as she approached.

"That's quite all right. You left me alone in the swamp last night. I'd rather go by myself."

His eyes narrowed. "I knew you were capable of finding your way back to the house."

"Thank you," she said dryly.

"Randal's rally is this morning. Both he and Jeanne will be there along with some of the store owners who knew your mother."

"Great." She walked toward Martha's old sky-blue sedan.

"I have to see Randal anyway. There's no reason for us both to drive in separately."

She kept walking. Yes, there was; she didn't want to be alone in the car with him.

"Do you know how to get there?"

She stopped. He had her there.

He stepped up behind her. "Although I believe you'll find no one has seen your mother in years."

She spun around, facing him. "If you believe that, then why the pretense of wanting to help me?"

He reached out and gently ran his fingertips along her jaw. She stiffened. She felt unsure and annoyed even as awareness tingled through her.

"I just don't want anything to happen to you," he said, his eyes tender, his voice soft.

Was that it? She wished she could trust him. She wanted to trust him, but just because he acts like he cares for a nanosecond doesn't mean he actually does.

He arched a brow. "Well?"

"All right," she agreed. There really was no reason to take two cars into town; she just hoped she wouldn't regret it later. She took Martha's keys back to her.

As they drove down the road with neither one talking, Laura stared out the window to keep from looking at him. His cologne permeated the air. She couldn't ignore it any more than she could ignore the imprint of his touch still lingering on her jaw. He had an intense physical affect on her and yet, she couldn't help wondering, if he wanted to help her, to be around her, then why was he so insistent she leave?

Could she trust anyone? Someone had lied to her, called her on the phone and brought her here promising the one thing she'd always longed for and hadn't had—her mother. It was cruel. And according to Drew, it was dangerous.

She had to find someone who'd known her mother, who'd been close to her, someone who could help her discover what had happened to her all those years ago.

They drove across Devil's Walk Bridge that stretched across the bayou and passed by the large white manor house she'd seen earlier from the cab.

"That's Randal and Jeanne's place," Drew said.

The Larames.

"I'd like to talk to them. They are the closest people to family I have." Her mother had been married to their son. They had to know something about her, maybe even something that could help Laura find her.

"What do you remember about Paul?" Drew's voice didn't sound quite right.

She turned to him. He was looking straight ahead though a muscle twitched in his jaw.

She thought back to her adopted father, and tried to bring up his face, but had trouble.

"I can't get a clear image, but I remember his smile and how much I cared for him."

An uneasy silence stretched between them. Laura shifted in her seat, wondering if there was something about Paul she should remember. They passed a man standing off to her right, his weathered face gaunt with chiseled narrowness, his eyes sunk deep into his skull. Spindly arms hung limp at his sides. In one hand he clutched a dead animal with a long, hairless tail; in the other he held a rusty hatchet. He watched her as they passed; his cold, hard gaze boring into her made her skin crawl.

"What is that man doing?" she blurted, louder than she'd intended.

"Possum hunting."

Laura watched the man step onto a flatboat and drift silently across the glassy waters back toward

Lionsheart. He tilted his head toward her in a slight nod. The gesture puckered the flesh on her arm.

The road widened slightly and they entered a small town. Drew parked the car then gestured toward the quaint shops surrounding a grassy town square. A large gazebo sat in the middle of the square.

"So what do you think? The town hasn't changed much—do you remember it at all?" Drew asked.

Laura looked around her but felt nothing. She squashed her disappointment. She couldn't expect all her memories to come back so soon. "It's very charming. Much more so than I'd expected."

"How about we stop at Mabel's Diner. You must remember Mabel's milk shakes?"

She didn't. "You're trying to cheer me up."

"I am."

Her gaze perused his face as she tried to understand him, but she could read nothing behind his guarded eyes.

He held out his hand. Hesitantly, she took it. Warmth spread through her at his touch. How could her body respond to him even when her mind warned her not to? They passed a sewing shop, an antiques store and a barbershop as they walked toward the small diner. Now that she was back in civilization, the air wasn't as cloying, nor did everything seem so sinister.

Even Drew didn't seem so dangerous. Perhaps she was jumping at shadows that didn't exist.

"Your mom used to bring us down here to play in the park." Drew waved toward a small park across the street.

She scanned the weathered playground equipment and the gazebo, wishing something looked familiar. It would be nice to be able remember her mom pushing her on the swings or spinning her on the merry-go-round, rather than living with this dark empty hole of nothingness.

She looked at Drew's hand clasped within her own. To the casual bystander it must look like the most natural thing in the world to be walking down the street, holding hands, going to get a milk shake.

When in fact, it was so surreal she could barely comprehend it.

Drew opened the door to the diner. She walked in and was immediately taken in by the old-fashioned red vinyl booths and the long soda counter forming a horseshoe around the kitchen.

An older woman with the name Mabel embroidered on her shirt approached them, rubbing her hands on her apron.

Perhaps this woman knew her mother.

Mabel's gaze caught Laura's. The woman stopped short, a look of stunned disbelief fixed on her face as her mouth dropped open.

Laura stiffened, her friendly smile freezing.

"Jesus, Mary and Joseph," Mabel said, crossing herself. "What are *you* doing here?"

Drew stepped forward. "Mabel, it's Laura Larame. Don't you remember her? She's come home."

Laura looked at him then back to Mabel. *No, not home.*

Mabel stared hard at Laura another second before her expression changed into guarded wariness.

"I'm looking for my mother, Delilah Larame," Laura said, annoyed when her voice broke.

Mabel's eyes widened. Her mouth hardened. "That woman ain't showed her face round these parts in a long time."

Stunned by the venom in her voice, Laura steeled herself for the confrontation. "Why not? What happened?"

"She's a murderer, that's why." Mabel's face reddened and spittle formed around the corners of her mouth. "That's what happened!"

Laura gasped, her eyes widening.

"And if you find her, you send her back this way so I can get me some justice for what she did to my Georgette."

Her nasty tone turned Laura's blood to ice as a chill swept through to her bones.

"*Merde,* Mabel. It was an accident. A tragedy for both our families."

"Was it? You Larames are the only ones who think so."

With a hand to the small of her back, Drew led

Laura out of the diner. They stood on the sidewalk as Laura tried to gather herself.

"You all right?" Drew asked.

No, she wasn't all right. "What was she talking about? What accident?"

"The one that killed Paul. Mabel's eighteen-year-old daughter, Georgette, was in the car with him. They both died instantly."

"And she thinks my mother had something to do with it?"

"The townspeople here can be a little strange. They're a superstitious lot who are always expecting the sky to fall. But like I said, it was an accident, nothing more."

"Then why did she call my mother a murderer?" She searched his eyes, trying to determine how much he was keeping from her. There had to be more. Before she could say another word, an elderly couple heading for the diner stopped and stared at her, their faces filling with trepidation. The woman clutched her husband's arm, and he hurried past her inside Mabel's place.

The fine hair on Laura's neck prickled. "People are looking at me like I kill puppies or something. Is it because of my mother? Because I look like her? What aren't you telling me? And why did you bring me here if you knew how people were going to react?"

"I haven't been here in a decade. I could only guess how people would respond. Many here believe Delilah killed Paul and Georgette. It's one of the reasons you shouldn't stay. Why people won't be too happy to see you, to remember the past. You needed to see that."

Be careful. Not everyone will want you here.

To Laura's dismay, she began to tremble, though she didn't know if it was from anger or pure emotional exhaustion. Drew stepped forward and pulled her against him. She didn't want to stand within his arms. He said he wanted to help her, but at every turn he did the exact opposite. Stiff in his embrace, she knew she should pull away, she should turn and run, but instead, she stood still, clinging to him until the warmth of his skin, the smell of his cologne, the feel of his strong, hard *male* body reached inside her. She relaxed as his hands moved lightly up and down her back, sending erotic shivers cascading through her.

She blew out a deep sigh. "You're right. My mother couldn't still be living here surrounded by all this animosity." Laura looked around her, searching the faces of people passing by and found nothing to welcome her. The small town had lost its charm, its quaintness, and instead had become something ugly.

Drew's bayou-green eyes held hers. "People here have had more than their share of tragedy for a small town. It's made them wary and suspicious. Are you going to be okay? Do you want to go back?"

"I'm fine. And no, I don't want to go back. Not

yet." She forced a smile and, though she was reluctant, she let him go. Why was it he suddenly seemed to be the only normal person in a world gone insane?

And he didn't want her there. She took a step toward the curb and glanced across the street at the park he'd said they used to play in as children. She tried to recall happier, more innocent times, when she was young and her mother was there to watch out for her.

"There must have been a reason she left you behind," he said against her hair, standing close behind her. Was it the heat of his breath or the deep timbre of his voice that caused her heart to race?

"I only hope I can discover what that reason was."

A child laughed as her mother pushed her high on the swing.

Because mothers who love their children don't abandon them.

A large white Mercedes passed them and pulled up next to the town square. Drew blew out a breath as he glanced at his watch. "They're early."

Laura stared at the top-of-the-line car and her stomach flip-flopped. *The Larames.* Would they remember her? Would they be pleased to see her? Or would she remind them of her mother? She hoped they didn't blame her mother for Paul's death, too.

With a gentle touch on her arm, Drew led her across the street toward the car. "Randal's running for senator again and he's holding a small pep rally. Not that he needs to. He already has this town's votes."

"Do you think they'll be happy to see me?" Whatever they felt, she hoped they didn't look at her in shocked disbelief and fear like the rest of the townspeople.

"I think they'll definitely be surprised."

As they approached the car, the driver's door opened and a well-dressed man stepped onto the pavement. Drew shifted in front of her, blocking her from the man's view.

"Hello, Randal," Drew said, stepping forward.

"Drew!" Randal grabbed Drew's offered hand and pulled him into a warm embrace. "It's good to see you."

Over Drew's shoulder, Randal was grinning from ear to ear and patting Drew's back, until his gaze caught Laura's. Randal's hand froze in midpat. His mouth dropped open. Slowly, he stepped back from Drew then moved to the side to get a better look at her. Which allowed her to get a better look at him.

The first thing that struck her was how tall he was, how polished. He moved with a poise and regal demeanor that set him apart and begged to be noticed. His suit was cut to fit his form perfectly and portray worldly elegance and Southern charm. He was in great shape and sported a full head of thick, silver hair that lent him an air of distinction.

This was a man of power, a man used to getting

his way. Laura couldn't help but feel intimidated by the intensity of his gaze. Especially when his eyes, dark and deep-set, hardened and fixated on her. There was nothing familiar about him, yet as he stood there staring at her, a wave of unreasonable fear broke over her, tensing her muscles and turning her stomach. Before either of them could utter a word, the car's passenger door swung open and Laura heard a loud gasp.

"Goodness me, is that our Laura?" A petite, dark-haired woman in an expensive taupe suit stepped out of the car, her eyes widening in shock as her hand rose to cover her mouth.

"Hello, Jeanne," Drew said. "Yes, Laura's come back."

The woman ran around the front of the car toward her, her arms opened wide and tears glistening in her eyes. "Oh, Laura. My God, I would have known you anywhere. You've grown up to be so beautiful, just like your mama."

The small woman almost knocked Laura off her feet as she pulled her into a big hug. She seemed happy to see her. Really, truly happy!

Smiling, Laura relaxed as her unwarranted fear dissipated.

"She's the spitting image of her mama, isn't she, Randal?" Jeanne said.

Randal stepped toward them, his lips widening into a smile that did not reach his winter-gray eyes.

"Welcome home, Laura," he said with as much practiced phony sincerity as a politician could muster. In fact, Laura might have even believed he'd meant it, if she hadn't seen the blood drain from his face the moment he'd laid eyes on her.

Laura felt Drew's hand on the small of her back and couldn't help the rush of warmth spreading through her.

"And, Drew, it's wonderful to see you back home again. Look at you, you must be six feet tall! I'm getting a crimp in my neck just looking at you," Jeanne said, laughing.

She had a nice laugh, genuine and lighthearted. A warm tug of recognition filled Laura.

"Come on, honey," Jeanne said, and grabbed Laura's arm. "Let's go get you a Southern treat. I bet you haven't had a praline since you left us."

As Jeanne swept her along, Laura tried not to notice that everywhere she looked, people were staring at them. They stopped in front of a small stand where a young man was selling large pecan clusters.

"Two, please," Jeanne said, and handed one to Laura.

Laura took a bite of the soft candy and was surprised by the incredible burst of butter and brown sugar. "Oh, this is good," she murmured and took another bite.

The teen selling the candy stared at her, his eyes

narrowing as if trying to remember how he knew her. But he couldn't know her. He was too young.

Something brushed up against her leg. Laura looked down and saw a large blue ball next to her foot. A little girl with Goldilocks curls and a wide cheeky grin came running toward her, her arms outstretched. Laura smiled, bent down and picked up the ball, holding it in outstretched arms.

"Isn't she just adorable?" Jeanne said.

"Ball," the toddler demanded.

Laura laughed and placed the ball in her arms. Running toward them, a woman scooped up the child so fast she began to wail. Stunned, Laura glanced up at the mother and was horrified to see fear contorting the woman's face. Clutching her toddler against her chest, she turned and hurried away.

"Come on, sweetie," Jeanne said, and patted Laura's shoulder.

Laura stood, her gaze tracking the fleeing mother and child. "What was that about?"

"Who knows? First-time mothers can be ridiculously overprotective."

They were halfway across the street when Jeanne stopped and turned. "You coming, Drew?" she called.

Laura didn't hear his answer. Like the little girl so fascinated with her ball, Laura was spellbound by crystals and faeries hanging in the window of a small shop directly across the street. Several primitive dolls with large black empty eye sockets sunk in skeletal heads lined the picture window, their stick bodies liberally decorated with feathers, twine and rough-hewn cloth.

A thick sense of foreboding skittered along Laura's spine. "Are those voodoo dolls?"

The lace curtains behind the door moved and the stone-cold eyes of the shopkeeper bored into hers.

"You don't remember Voodoo Mystique? Mary and your mama used to be real close. Every time she'd take you for a visit, you'd come home with fairy dust sprinkled across your nose."

A friend of her mother's! Someone who might have the answers she needed, and yet, as Laura stared at the dark gaping holes where the doll's eyes should be, she couldn't seem to make herself move forward. Her legs felt frozen as an icy fear swept through her.

"Laura? Is everything all right?" Jeanne asked.

An engine revved to an ear-bursting roar drowned out Laura's reply. The squeal of tires gripping asphalt vibrated the ground beneath her feet.

Suddenly, a loud cracking convulsed through the air, sounding like shots being fired from the town's square behind them. People screamed and scattered, running and ducking for cover.

Laura and Jeanne hunched over, covering their ears. A large tan car raced down the street, barreling toward them. Laura's heart slammed into the side of her chest. Jeanne yanked on her arm.

They ran. Laura tripped and stumbled, falling. Asphalt bit into her knees and palms. She found herself alone in the driver's path. A scream caught in her throat.

"Laura!" Jeanne screamed.

Laura scrambled to her feet and ran for the sidewalk. The car sped past her. The door to Voodoo Mystique flew open and a small woman wearing a long, flowing purple dress grabbed Laura's arm and pulled her inside the shop's doorway.

Laura stared after the car, her heart pounding. Within seconds, Jeanne was by her side, her eyes widened with fear. "You okay, sweetie?"

As Laura shut the door, she couldn't seem to catch her breath and her palms stung from her brush with the pavement.

"He tried to run me down." She looked around her, scanning the room for the woman in purple. Where had she gone?

"No, no. It was an accident," Jeanne said. "Thank goodness you're okay." She patted Laura's shoulder. "You're okay," she repeated.

She had a funny look in her eyes, and Laura wasn't sure which one of them she was trying to convince.

Jeanne turned and peeked out the lace-covered window. "Did you hear all that racket? What in the name of heaven is going on out there? I don't see Randal or Drew anywhere."

"Stay here," a voice from the shadows ordered. "Don't you go out there, Jeanne."

Laura's eyes adjusted and she made out the shape of a small woman standing in the corner. Laura tried to get a better look at her, but the woman stepped deeper into the shadows and Laura couldn't make out her features in the gloom.

"Thank you for your help." Laura stepped forward but stopped as she noticed several grotesque dolls hanging suspended from the ceiling above her head.

A tight band encircled her chest squeezing off her breath. Images of horror surrounded her. Skulls of various animals, jars filled with hair, teeth and other weird-looking items lined the wall next to her. Bones, feathers, snake skins and alligator heads filled bookshelves.

What was this place? She stepped back toward the door.

Drew burst in. "Is everyone all right?"

"How's Randal?" Again Jeanne peered out the window. "I can't see him."

"He's fine. He's in the car." Drew walked toward Laura. Concern heavy in his eyes. "How about you?"

A lump filled her throat, blocking her breath. She shook her head. She didn't know how she was. She didn't even know where she was. What kind of woman was her mother's friend?

Drew took her hands in his and lightly rubbed the scraped, reddened skin with his thumb. His gaze caught hers and her heart jumped. For a second she wished she could step into his arms and rest her head against his chest. If she could just feel his arms around her, she knew his warmth would chase away the darkness surrounding her.

But the thought was crazy. This man wasn't her friend. And he wasn't pretending to be.

Jeanne turned from the window. "Drew, I heard shots. Was someone shooting out there?"

"Firecrackers." He dropped Laura's hands and turned to Jeanne.

Laura crossed her arms over her chest and held herself tight to keep from pulling him back, to keep from bolting.

"Firecrackers? That's absurd," Jeanne said, her voice rising. "Who would do that?"

Everywhere Laura turned she saw gaping black holes in faceless skulls. Why did they scare her so much? She had to get out of there.

"Someone who wanted to distract us from the car that almost ran Laura down," Drew answered. "Did either of you get a good look at the driver?"

Laura's attention snapped back to Drew. Had someone tried to kill her? Who? Why?

Because they don't want you here. The voice from that strange phone call echoed in her head.

She swayed, feeling unsteady on her feet.

Drew stepped closer and wrapped a steady arm around her waist. "Are you all right?" he asked softly.

She nodded, not trusting herself to speak. Instead, she clung to him, smelling his spicy scent, feeling his strength and remembering what it was like to have him hold up her world.

But they weren't kids anymore.

"No one even knows Laura is here," Jeanne argued. "Lighting firecrackers sounds like teenagers stirring things up and messing around. I'm sure it has nothing to do with Laura or the car."

"You're probably right." Drew dropped his arm from Laura's waist and joined Jeanne at the window.

Laura reached for him then pulled back. She couldn't use him as a shield against this evil place. She had to get through this on her own. She had to face it if she was going to find out the truth about what happened to her mother, and if she was even alive.

Light flickered against the glass eyes of a reptile. Laura hated mysticism. Hated the tarot card readers that lined Haight Street in San Francisco, the palm readers who promised good fortune, the so-called psychics who could predict the future. She'd never wanted anything to do with any of it, and yet, here she stood in a den of evil.

And it was a place frequented by her mother.

"Besides," Jeanne continued. "Why would someone want to run Laura down? Folks around here can be a little skittish, but just because she looks like her mama that's hardly a reason to run someone down in the road."

"Revenge is always a reason." The small woman still lurking in the shadows finally stepped forward. "They don't want *her* here."

The woman's words reached inside Laura and clamped a bony hold on her heart. She looked to Drew, who was suddenly standing next to the door as if he, too, wanted to get as far away from her as possible.

"Revenge? What has Laura ever done to anyone?" Jeanne's voice sounded loud and shrill in the small shop.

"Not Laura. Delilah," the woman said. "For killing Paul and Georgette."

Laura thought back to what Drew had said about the accident. She recalled her adopted father's easy smile and wide, loving arms. She'd loved him. Her mother had loved him. Everyone had. What this woman said couldn't possibly be true.

Jeanne's eyes narrowed and her tone deepened. "Mary, I don't want to hear that. Delilah did not kill my son. It was an accident. A horrible accident. You know that."

Before Mary could respond, the door opened again. The tinkling of the bells echoed throughout the room and through Laura's mind. Memories clicked into focus—the smell of sandalwood incense, her mother and Mary talking in hushed whispers, chanting as their fingers worked magic with the dolls.

Voodoo dolls.

Laura shivered as a bone-deep chill shook her. Randal stepped into the shop and Jeanne rushed to him. Laura stared into Mary's black gaze, and watched it narrow. Yes, she remembered what Mary and her mother had done in this shop on those hot, summer nights so long ago. And Mary knew she knew. She could see the certainty burning like hot embers within the depths of her dark Creole eyes.

Had her mother and this woman killed Papa Paul? The thought sliced painfully through Laura's heart. Was that why her mother had disappeared and never returned?

"The rally's about to start," Randal said.

Jeanne nodded and without another word they walked out the door.

Before Laura could join them, Mary shoved a little bag into Laura's palm and squeezed her hand over it. "Trust no one," she whispered, her big dark eyes rounding with dead seriousness. Laura's stomach plummeted. She pulled her hand away and turned to Drew who stood in the doorway watching them. For a split second, Laura thought she saw fear shining in his eyes.

He was afraid? Of what?

And then she knew. As she held the lump of fabric clutched in her cold grasp, she knew that he was afraid, that, like her mother, she would disappear, too.

Chapter 5

Drew stood outside the doorway of Voodoo Mystique and wished he could step out into the street, into the light, away from the gloom. The spirits were all around Laura, hovering, surrounding…protecting? He wished he knew.

All his life he'd worked hard at blocking them. It'd been years since he could hear them, and he'd thought he'd reached the point where he no longer saw them. Life had been good.

Until he'd come back here.

Until Laura.

He should jump on the nearest plane and hightail it back to Atlanta. Back to his empty house. But he knew he wouldn't be able to sleep at night knowing he'd left her here. Knowing she was destined to end up in the swamp, which was probably what had happened to Delilah, and certainly what had happened to Paul.

Destiny, like death, was hard to fight.

Laura walked unsteadily out of Mary's shop. Her face was ashen, her eyes wide and slightly dazed. He stepped forward and took her by the arm, suddenly angry that he was stuck in this impossible situation. Why couldn't she just leave?

"Come on, Laura. Let's go back to the house."

She looked up at him and nodded.

Her arm felt small in his hand, her bones fragile within his strong grasp. She was just a wisp of a girl. She had no chance out here. Not against the darkness or the power that was death.

The old familiar feeling of defeat washed over him, making him clench her arm harder. He should tell her everything he knew and drive her directly to the airport, without stopping, without looking back.

Chances were she wouldn't believe him. He wished he didn't believe.

Jeanne hurried toward them. "It's almost time for Randal to give his speech. Come sit with me."

Laura stiffened.

"I'm sorry, Jeanne, but I think we should get back to the house," Drew said, at once thankful not to have to play nice nephew and sit through the rally. Coming here had been a mistake. It was time to cut this visit short.

Disappointment filled Jeanne's face. "All right. I'll see you later," she said to Laura, then hugged them both.

Drew settled Laura in the car, then walked around it and got into the driver's seat.

She held out a fist clenched so tightly her knuckles were white. "Take it please," she said, thrusting her hand toward him.

He pulled her fingers open revealing a small felt pouch that had been crushed within her grasp. He took it, and she immediately yanked her hand back and rubbed it vigorously against her jeans.

Dread worried the pit of his stomach.

"What is it?" Laura asked.

"It's juju." The colorful square bag had been completely stitched around the perimeter forming a small pillow decorated with buttons, feathers and ribbons. He wanted to throw it out the window, but instead pulled open the stitches and spread the contents in his hand. Herbs, dried blossoms, roots, nuts and feathers spread across his palm, still warm from her grip on them.

He poked through the items and pulled out a bone. "A protection spell," he said aloud, though he couldn't be sure. He hadn't seen the contents of a juju since he was young. Since he'd been forced to learn his spells the way other kids learned their catechism.

"Protection? From what?"

He turned to her and peered into her eyes, willing

her to understand. "From the forces that want to hurt you."

"Why would anyone want to hurt me? No one even knows I'm here. At least they didn't until I came to this freaky town," she mumbled.

Drew sighed and dumped the contents in his palm back into the pouch and placed it between the seats on the console then shifted in his seat so he was facing her. It was time to try a different tactic.

"Laura, someone lied to bring you here, and now you were almost run over in the street." He took her hand in his, and stroked her soft skin with the pad of his thumb. "You should go home. It isn't safe for you here."

He read the warring emotions wrestling for position within the depths of her eyes. She was afraid, and yet she was determined to finish what she started.

"If I leave now, I'll always wonder what happened to my mother. Where did she go? Is she still alive? I need proof one way or another."

He understood how she felt, even if he didn't like it.

"And why would my mother be involved with something like voodoo?" She gestured toward the juju.

That was easy.

"When you grow up in the swamp, in a town like this one, voodoo is as much a part of your life as gumbo and crawfish étouffée. It's in our blood. It's who we are."

Laura visibly shuddered.

"It's why you should leave the search for your mother to someone who knows these people and their customs. Contrary to popular belief, not all voodoo is evil, nor are all the people who practice it."

She turned to him, her eyes wide. "Do *you* practice it?"

"No. But I'm not afraid of it.

"It had been a part of my life when I was growing up. And yours, too, for a little while. Apparently you don't remember."

Laura stared at him with surprise widening her eyes. "All I know is that when I see items of the occult or I'm in a shop like Voodoo Mystique, I feel evil touching me. It scares me."

"Mary was your mother's best friend. Most likely she has the answers you're looking for. Go home. I'll talk to her, find out what she knows."

"That's all right. I'll talk to Mary. Just not right now."

"Then when?" he pressed.

"What about my mom's stuff? Is any of it left at the house?" she countered.

Drew turned back in his seat so he was facing forward and rested his hands on the steering wheel, deliberately, casually, as anxiety tightened his chest.

"Maybe looking at her things will help jog some of my memories," she continued. "Then I'll talk to Mary."

He was not going up there.

"I suppose I should ask your mom. She could probably show me."

"In the attic," he said, pushing the words past clenched teeth. Better to leave his *mère* out of it.

"What?"

"Your mother's things. They're in the attic."

Excitement flared across her face. "Great! Let's go."

Damn.

While Drew went searching for Martha in her private rooms that she kept in the back wing of the house to confirm her mother's things were still in the attic, Laura headed up to her room. She hesitated at the top of the stairs when she spotted her mother's door at the end of the hall. If she could just force herself to enter that room, maybe more of her memories would come back to her.

And maybe if she remembered, she could go home.

She focused on her mother's door at the end of the hall and hurried toward it, even as her stomach tightened and churned. No more being a wimp. She had to get through that door. Chances were there was nothing even in there. The only thing holding her back was her stupid fear. And there was nothing to be afraid of. She took a deep breath and willed her insides to calm.

She could do this. She had to do this. If something had happened in that room, something she'd buried in her mind, she was going to have to pull it out and face it or she'd never remember.

A cramp sliced through her stomach. She clutched at it, but continued forward. Almost there, she told herself. No need to stop now. Five feet. Three feet. She could almost feel the doorknob in her hand. She could do it this time. She *would* do it this time.

Beads of sweat formed on her forehead and rolled into her eyes, blurring her vision. If she could just get through her mother's door then everything would be okay. She knew it. She'd be able to breathe. The pain would cease and everything would be as it should be.

She'd remember what had happened in that room and she'd know why her mother had left her all alone. She'd know her mother hadn't left because of her. Because she hadn't been good enough.

Or loved enough.

Stopping in front of the door, Laura took a deep breath and curved her hand around the knob. The knob's metal seared her palm. Shooting pain shot up her arm. Yelping, she yanked her hand back. The acrid scent of burning flesh filled her nose. A stinging throb pulsated through her. In shocked disbelief she watched raw blisters rise on her skin.

Tears swam in her eyes. She stared at the ugly, oozing burns then fell back against the wall, clutching her hand to her chest, her eyes squeezed shut.

How could a doorknob burn her hand?

Slowly, the pain faded. Laura opened her eyes and looked once more at her palm. Horror rolled over her as the blisters began to disappear. The bright red tinge dulled until finally her hand returned to normal.

She rubbed her hand where the blisters had been but felt no pain, not even the slightest sensitivity.

How was that possible? Was she losing her mind? This house, this place... She turned back to her mother's door. Something was very wrong here.

Laura heard someone coming up the stairs. She turned and saw Drew step onto the landing and walk toward her down the hall. She looked back down at her hand. The marks were gone, her palm, smooth.

She wanted to say something, but what could she say? How could she explain the unexplainable? It couldn't be real. She glanced back at her mother's door and reached for it, her hand hovering over the knob. But she couldn't make herself touch it. Not again.

Was she going crazy?

She turned back to Drew and, for a second, he had that same pinched look he'd had earlier, then the coldness touched his eyes. Warning bells clanged in the back of her mind.

Was anything in this house what it seemed?

He stopped in front of her. "You sure you don't want to rest awhile?"

Was that hope she heard in his voice? Or concern? She looked at her palm once more, debating whether or not to tell him what happened, but decided it was too bizarre. "No, I'm ready."

"All right. The attic is this way." He gestured down the hall and gave her a hesitant crooked smile that was both boyish and charming. For a second, as she looked at him, she forgot the uncertainties ringing in her mind.

But only for a second.

He placed a guiding hand on her arm. She wondered why his touch and his silly crooked smile would affect her the way it did. And why, for just that second, the sadness and the fear disappeared along with the absolute certainty that she was losing her grip on reality.

They reached the far door at the end of the hall. Drew's shoulders tensed and his face paled.

Fear nudged her. "What is it?"

"I—uh—should have brought a flashlight. You'll be all right here a minute?"

"Of course. But are you sure everything is okay?" She got the distinct impression his hesitation had nothing to do with a flashlight.

"Fine."

"Okay," she muttered, and watched him walk back down the hall.

While he was gone, Laura studied the attic door and its worn brass knob. Should she chance touching it? Somehow it seemed as if the house itself was trying to stop her from discovering the truth about her mother.

Drawing a deep breath, she brushed the tip of a finger across the knob's surface. Cold. Quickly, she grasped it, turned then yanked the door open. Pulling her hand back, she exhaled a relieved breath and peered up the darkened narrow stairwell.

There was nothing sinister here, nothing to be afraid of. She flicked the light switch on the wall to her right. Nothing happened. She glanced up at the old bulb in the ceiling and flicked the switch again. The wooden steps lay hidden in dark shadows. The bulb must need replacing. No wonder Drew wanted a flashlight. But it really wasn't that far to the top, and there was plenty of light filling the narrow corridor through the opened door behind her.

Frowning, Laura stepped inside and up a couple steps. She should wait for Drew. She knew that, but instead she climbed a couple more. Then another. An icy breeze touched her cheek. Her heart stilled. Behind her, the door swung shut, throwing the stairwell into pitch darkness.

Shit! Laura spun toward the door, but saw only

darkness. She took a deep breath to calm her nerves, then eased her way back down the stairs. After reaching the last step, she felt for the knob. Groping along the door, running her hands across the entire surface, she searched but found nothing.

Where was the knob?

"Hello? Drew!" She pounded on the door.

Nothing.

Then she heard something behind her. A step on the stairs. She froze. When it didn't come again, she continued her perusal of the door.

Then she heard a scratch along the wall.

Knowing it was useless, she turned to look behind her.

She felt something—a presence in the darkness. All around her. Smothering her. Panic scraped the edges of her nerves. She tried to concentrate on listening, but couldn't hear a thing over the roar of blood rushing through her ears.

She turned back to the door and pushed at it, trying to force her way out.

"Drew!"

Another step. She pounded on the door. Scratched. Her fingernail snapped. Behind her a loose board squeaked and echoed in the stairwell.

Then a thump.

Thump.

Thump.

"Drew!" Laura hit the door with both fists.

A light touch skittered across the back of her neck. She screamed.

The door flew open.

She fell forward, stumbling into Drew's arms. She clung to his shoulders, gulping in deep breaths, trying to still her racing heart, and block her panicky tears.

"What happened?" Drew pulled back and placed his hand under her chin, tilting her face up to his. "You're shaking."

"I couldn't get the door open. I...I heard something."

Something was in there with me.

He looked down into her eyes, and there it was again—that concerned look. He was worried about her. *She* was worried about her. What was going on in this house?

What was going on with her?

"Why didn't you wait for me?" he demanded.

Was he angry?

"I...I was curious. Everything was fine until the door blew shut." She shivered and looked behind her toward the attic door.

It was closed again. Had it blown shut?

She *hadn't* imagined something in there with her. Had she?

Drew stepped away from her and opened the attic door. A baseball bounced down the last few steps and came to rest between his feet.

A ball?

"Oh my God," she cried, choking on a laugh. "That must be what I heard. I was afraid of a baseball."

Drew wasn't smiling. In fact, he didn't say anything, just stood there staring at the ball.

Her smile died. "It's okay. Really. Isn't it?"

He stepped over the ball and turned toward the door. "This door opens with a latch, right here." He showed her a latch built into the top of the door. "If it shuts on you again, just pull it, and the door will swing open."

"I felt over the whole door and didn't feel that latch." *I should have felt that latch.*

"These old houses can be spooky."

There was an unfamiliar tension in his voice. And he wasn't looking her in the eyes. Something was definitely wrong. A shudder moved through her.

Drew peered up the stairwell. "These old houses are always creaking and shifting. That's probably what you heard."

"That and the ball. I wonder how a ball got lodged at the top of the stairs?"

His lips thinned as his jaw tightened. He turned on the flashlight and stepped into the stairwell. Laura stared after him, reluctant to follow. Something was bothering him and he wasn't sharing. She rubbed the back of her neck. She might not want to believe it, but she hadn't imagined that icy touch. Something had been in that stairwell with her.

Drew turned, his face ghostly pale in the wan light.

"Are you coming?" he asked.

No!

She pushed the protest aside and nodded, then climbed toward him up the stairs.

Chapter 6

Laura followed Drew into the darkened attic and stood in awe as he swung the beam of the flashlight over boxes, pictures, clothes, hats—years' worth of dusty discarded items.

"Look how many of these boxes have my mother's name written on them." Laura hurried past him toward the boxes. She fought an urge to sit on the floor and start digging through her mother's life, searching for answers. "Why would she leave all this stuff here?"

Drew shrugged and walked into a shaft of waning sunlight streaming from a window covered with years of dust and spiderwebs.

"Look over here." He gestured toward large bolts

of fabric hung on racks fastened to the wall next to an old sewing machine.

Laura approached a large bin full of faceless rag dolls. Heartache squeezed her chest as she picked up one of the small eight-inch dolls. She ran her fingers over the tiny yellow yarn braids. "I remember these. She called them pocket dolls. I still have one that I took with me when I went to live in San Francisco."

"I don't remember her making the dolls."

She looked up at him. The tension that had hardened the lines around his eyes seemed to dissipate as he stared into the bin. "Why would you?"

"Your mother meant a lot to me when I was growing up. I missed her when she left." His gaze held hers. "I missed you both."

He'd missed her? He'd thought about her? She wanted to hold him, to rest her head against his chest, to feel his heart beating, and smell his warm male scent.

But she couldn't.

Something was going on with him. Something that scared her.

Come on, Drew, make a move.

They stared at each other until an awkward tension stretched between them.

Drew turned away. He couldn't seem to stop himself. He couldn't be there for her. He couldn't let himself get close to her. It didn't matter that he wanted to spend more time with her, to see how far their connection would take them. They had no future together, because she had no future. Damn him for an idiot.

He watched her walk around the attic touching her mother's things, her soft cotton blouse clinging to her body, outlining her breasts. If he closed his eyes he could still smell her light scent, and feel her soft touch. She was beautiful, desirable with her long dark hair dancing around her shoulders. And when her eyes met his...his heart skipped.

He wished he could stop watching her, stop thinking about her. Stop wanting her. For her sake he hoped Delilah was out there somewhere. But what were the odds? Mothers usually didn't run out on their kids and disappear for twenty years.

Unless something terrible happened to make them.

Something terrible was going to happen to Laura if he didn't get her away from there.

Laura knelt down, her hands trembling as she opened another box. Drew turned away. Reluctantly he walked toward the shadows in the back of the room, his gut twisting with each step. He hated it up here, always had. He could remember the odd sounds reverberating from the ceiling in his room—the pounding, the chanting. And then there was the time he'd gotten out of bed to investigate an odd smell that had drifted down the hall from the opened attic door and sickened his stomach. He'd thrown up, and his mother had kept the door locked from then on.

He played his flashlight beam over the darkened corner then entered another room. Paul stood in front of him. Only this time he wasn't holding Drew's old baseball and he wasn't smiling. His face was twisted in anger, even as his eyes widened with desperation.

He lunged forward and seized Drew's arm. Horrified, Drew tried to pull back, to shake him loose, but Paul's grip was too tight. Images filled Drew's mind: Candles flickering, black smoke rising through the air, the overpowering scent of incense. Randal holding a squirming eight-year-old Laura down. Dousing her forehead with some kind of oil. And blood.

So much blood.

"Drew, what is that?" Laura's voice, her slight touch, brought him reeling back from the vision.

He faltered. Laura grabbed hold of him.

Paul was gone.

"Are you all right?" Her large blue eyes bored into his.

He let himself get lost in them, and then it seemed things would be okay…for a moment.

"Drew?"

He straightened. "Yes, fine." But he wasn't fine and from the look on her face, he knew he wasn't fooling her. The visions Paul had shown him, they were from that night he and Laura almost drowned. What had Randal done to her?

"I don't like it up here," he admitted.

"I can see why." She nodded toward a table covered with a long white cloth. It held several thick, half-burned candles of different shapes and colors, and a scattering of statues of what looked like Catholic saints. Dried herbs and dead flowers hung upside down, dropping small pieces to litter the cloth.

Drew's stomach turned.

"Do you smell that?" she asked.

"What?" He didn't smell anything other than years of dust and stale air, and perhaps the faint hint of incense.

"Nothing," she whispered, but he could tell she was hiding something from him. He thought of the way she'd reacted at her mother's door, and earlier in the stairwell with the ball. For the second time, he couldn't help wondering if perhaps this house and the spirits in it were having an effect on her. If maybe she was a touch intuitive herself.

"It's a voodoo altar, isn't it?" Her voice broke.

"Yes."

To his surprise, she stepped toward the table. He placed a hand on her arm to stop her. Suddenly he didn't want her to remember. To *touch* it.

"You don't have to go near it."

"But I do. If I want to find my mother, I'm going to

have to face my fears and remember what happened to us."

For an instant, he wanted to tell her, to reveal the horrible truth of that night, at least what he could remember from what Paul had shown him. But he couldn't seem to make himself form the words.

He followed her to the altar and watched her gaze take in the scattered herbs and spilled candle wax; the dried, severed alligator head and the chicken feathers strewn haphazardly around the floor.

"Is that blood?" she asked.

The few drops on the cloth did look like blood. "Most likely rooster or some other animal blood." He hoped.

She looked up at him, her eyes wide and vulnerable and he stopped himself from pulling her into his arms and holding her tight. He knew he wouldn't be doing it for her, but for himself. He wanted so badly to hold her in his arms, to try and forget that horrible night. To do what he'd always done, to push it all out of his mind and move forward.

"Do you think this was my mother's altar?"

"Perhaps. They said she was a voodoo priestess. She and Mary ran Voodoo Mystique together." But he knew better. It hadn't been Delilah up here on those late dark nights. It had been his mother.

Laura grimaced. "What is a voodoo priestess, exactly?"

"A person who performs rituals and spells. The

altar could have been hers originally, but it doesn't look like it's been sitting here untouched all this time. That blood looks recent."

"Drew," she hesitated. "Do you think... Is it possible...?"

The hopeful tone of her voice said it all. "Do I think your mother is alive and hiding in the swamp?"

She nodded.

"No," he said. Brutal, blunt and honest. "Not without anyone seeing her all these years."

Laura sighed, and the hope shining in her eyes faded to disappointment. "I know. You're right. I guess I want her to be alive so much, I'm willing to believe anything."

"Family is a powerful thing."

She turned away from the altar and walked back toward her mother's boxes.

Suddenly, a thick, musky odor drifted through the air and he knew exactly what Laura had smelled earlier.

The scent of blood.

He left the altar and hurried back across the room.

Laura stopped in front of her mother's bins and pulled a small doll off the top. "From all the stuff my mother left behind, I don't believe she had planned on leaving here that night."

"It doesn't look like it."

Laura turned to him, her big blue eyes wide with

vulnerability. He hated it when she looked at him like that. She was too hard to resist, to turn away from.

"I'm afraid something bad happened to her."

"If that's true, the best thing you could do, the safest thing you could do, would be to get on a plane and go home."

"I know that. Deep in my gut, I know I should leave. But I just can't. Not yet. This is my last chance to discover the truth."

"You realize you might never find out why she left you."

"I know. But you have to understand, after I got that phone call, I allowed myself to hope, to imagine that she was alive and had been living out here all this time." Tears welled in her eyes and tore at his heart. "I've been such a fool."

He stepped forward and, against his better judgment, pulled her into his arms. She clung to him, nestling close. He burrowed his head in her hair and breathed deep her sweet scent. Her breasts pressed up against him, leaving him wanting so much more. He wanted to taste her lips, to feel their softness, to lose himself in her touch, her taste.

But he couldn't let her lean on him. If he did, then she'd stay. And then he wouldn't be able to stop what would happen. He wouldn't be able to save her from death.

"You're not a fool for wanting a family, but Laura, it isn't safe for you here. Most likely you will never find the answers you're searching for. There's a lot of swamp out there, a lot of ways to make someone disappear. Go home. Hire a detective if you must have answers, but please, leave here as soon as possible."

She stiffened in his arms. "I know leaving is the logical, rational thing to do. But I can't go. Not yet."

She stepped back from him, clutching the small doll in her hand. "I can't leave Louisiana until I know for sure whether or not my mother is dead."

Drew could tell by the stubborn tilt to her jaw that there would be no arguing with her. He sighed and picked up one of her mother's boxes. "Let's say we get out of this dusty attic and take a couple of these downstairs. We can go through them in your room."

"Sounds like a great idea."

She bent over to pick up a box. Her blouse opened revealing soft, ample breasts cupped in white lace. Heat rolled through him. He took a deep breath to calm his racing thoughts, then followed her down the stairs, close enough behind that he caught her scent—sweet and seductive. He tried to ignore it, even as his blood pumped through him, heightening his senses, making him acutely aware of her every movement. He had to stop thinking about her that way. She could never be more than a friend to him.

A friend who was about to die.

He followed her into her room, flipped on the

light then set the box on the floor next to the French doors and settled next to it. He lifted the lid, not certain what he'd find, but fairly sure it wouldn't answer Laura's burning questions of what happened to Delilah.

Sitting across from him, Laura reached in and pulled out a flowery blouse. She held it under her nose, inhaling deeply.

"It's been a long time. It probably only smells of dust," he said.

"You're right." She smiled, a sad smile that tweaked something deep inside him. "So, tell me a little something about Drew," she said, digging deep into the bottom of her box.

He stiffened. There were so many things about himself that he could never share.

"Not much to tell. After you left here, this house got pretty quiet. There wasn't any more laughter, alligator hunts or water fights in the front yard."

"Sounds like we had fun." Her voice caught and she quickly turned away.

"What I'm saying is that I went away to boarding school not long after you left. And as hard as I'm sure San Francisco must have been for you back then, it really was better than being here in the swamp all by yourself."

"Maybe," Laura answered without meeting his gaze. She continued pulling sweaters out of the bottom of the box.

"Has your life been that...lonely?" he asked. He wasn't sure exactly what he was hoping to hear. He couldn't imagine a woman as beautiful as she was not having a line of men waiting for her back home.

Laura took a deep breath. "No, of course not. I have friends. A great job. Great boss."

"Boyfriends?"

She looked at him, meeting his gaze for a long moment. "There have been a few, but no one at the moment."

Relief loosened the tension in his shoulders, which concerned him even more. Her personal life shouldn't matter to him. "Hey, look at this," he said and held up a picture of the two of them as children wearing bathing suits and wide toothy grins.

"I remember that day," she said.

"You do?"

"Yes, your mom had given us ice cream and I'd gotten mine all over my bathing suit. She'd turned on the sprinklers and told us we weren't allowed back into the house until every speck of chocolate was gone." Laura smiled and stared at the picture.

He liked it when she smiled. Dammit, he had to get hold of himself.

"And Papa Paul brought us home that large plastic pool."

"Oh, yes," he said, surprised by the details she was able to recall. "Are your memories coming back?"

She looked pleased. "Little things here and there."

Her hand moved up his arm as she reached for the picture. Just a small trail gliding along his skin, and yet, the impact of her touch shook him to the core. He wanted her. More than he could remember ever wanting another woman.

She continued talking, rambling almost as if she was trying to pretend that they were two old friends reminiscing, that everything was normal...ordinary. When they both knew it wasn't. In an obvious attempt to put space between them, he shifted away.

"What about you?" she asked. "What has your life been like since you left here?"

"I'm a lawyer in Atlanta."

"I'm not surprised."

"Why is that?"

"Because when you get an idea in your head, you don't give up trying to prove your point." Her voice made a slight throaty sound.

"Is that right? And how would you know that?"

"Look how many times you've told me to go home." Her gaze focused on his lips.

He swallowed.

She moved closer.

"I'm worried about you," he defended. "I hope there's nothing wrong with that."

"No. Worry is good. I'll take it to mean you care." Again her gaze held his and his heart kicked up a beat. He should leave. Get up and go right now.

"I do care," he said, his voice sounding softer than he intended. "Which is why I think it would be wiser for you to pack up and go."

"I'm a big girl," she said with a slight curve to her luscious mouth. Her tongue slid out and moistened her lower lip.

He fought the images of what her tongue might feel like against his skin and took a deep breath to calm the heat rushing through his veins.

Laura leaned toward him. "A friend of mine recently told me that I need to stop letting life pass me by, that I need to take control of my own destiny. If I want something, I should go after it with all I've got."

His mouth went dry. "Sounds like good advice."

He had to get hold of himself.

He dug into the box hoping to find something to distract him from how closely she was sitting next to him, and how good she smelled. Longing rushed through him. She reached inside the box, too. Their fingers brushed. Their eyes met. He pulled away.

"Sometimes our destiny is chosen for us and there's not much we can do to change it," he said, his voice cracking. He couldn't stand the idea of not being able to see her again, of not being able to touch her. To see if this connection they had between them was real.

Her foot brushed against his. "Do you really believe that?"

Did he? "I think I'll go get another box."

"Okay. Me, too."

He stood. She bumped into him. She steadied herself, her hands braced against his chest. His arm wound around her waist to support her. Suddenly he was holding her against him, staring down into her face, looking at her full lips, wanting more than anything to dip his head and kiss her.

He didn't know who moved first, but before he had time to think his lips were smothering hers. She gave a soft whimper of pleasure, her palms flattening against his chest, her long hair brushing against his arms, tickling his skin.

His tongue swept the inside of her mouth, tasting, devouring. She pressed her body against his, her firm breasts pushing against his chest. Hunger pulsed through him. And a yearning that was almost more than he could bear.

He'd spent most of his life distancing himself from people, rarely getting close, and throwing all of his energy into his work. He didn't make time for relationships, for the simple pleasure of touch.

He couldn't take that chance.

He had never loved because he couldn't risk seeing the horror fill a woman's eyes the moment she found out the truth about him, when she discovered his curse. And this time was no different.

He pulled back, breaking free.

"I'm sorry," he said, and he was. Kissing Laura was a violation of everything he believed, everything he knew. She had a date with death and he could have no part of it.

Chapter 7

A few hours later, Laura had unpacked and repacked almost all of her mother's boxes and, unfortunately, had learned nothing new. She and Drew had decided earlier that after such a long day, a simple dinner would be best. She walked into the kitchen and found him sitting at the table by himself eating a bowl of soup.

"You should have called for me. I would have come earlier," she said, and pulled out a chair.

"I didn't want to bother you. Corn bread's in the oven." He stirred his soup and took another bite without looking up.

She walked toward the oven, slightly confused by his cool demeanor. "Where's your mom?"

"She took a bowl with her to her rooms down the hall." He gestured behind him, beyond the kitchen, without smiling or even looking at her. "She said she wanted to go bed early."

Laura stared at him for a moment. What was up with the sudden chill? She hadn't known why he apologized after he kissed her. She certainly hadn't minded. And quite a kiss it was. She was still feeling the effect of belly-meltdown.

Afterward, he'd brought down all the boxes from the attic then without saying another word, quickly excused himself. Apparently, their kiss hadn't affected him as strongly as it had her. She sighed then filled up a bowl of the soup and took a piece of corn bread out of the oven.

"Any ideas about what we should do tomorrow?" she asked, trying to engage him in a conversation, or at least get him to look at her.

"Get a good night's sleep." Drew's eyes met hers. "We'll brainstorm what to do next in the morning."

He got up, put his dishes in the dishwasher and left the room. She stared at his back as he retreated. Was it too much to hope for a smile? A hug? A good-night kiss?

Apparently.

Feeling disheartened and slightly sorry for herself, she quickly ate then took care of her own dishes and walked up the stairs. She hoped he would still help her with her search. When she finally remembered what had happened to her mother, she didn't want to be alone.

If she remembered. When she was a teenager, a doctor had tried putting her on some kind of drug to help her recall what had happened to her. The effect had been brutal, the nightmarish memories causing pain and torment. He quickly took her off the drugs. She had never tried to shake those memories loose again. Never wanted to.

Until now.

At the top of the stairs, she flipped on the light switch and illuminated the darkened hallway. She walked by her mother's pictures, but this time didn't look at them. Right now she didn't want to think about her mother or about what had happened. She didn't want nightmarish dreams or disjointed images to assail her sleep.

She stayed as far from the door to her mother's room as the wide hallway would allow and still, her heart kicked up a beat as she passed by it. Her strange reaction was unlike any she'd had before. The monster from her nightmares must live in that room and at some point she'd have to face it if she wanted to remember what happened.

Laura tripped on a frayed piece of carpet that had pulled loose and bounced off the wall. Drew was right. This house was old and moldy and, most of all, creepy. So far, meeting Drew again had been the high point of this whole trip.

She touched her fingers to her lips and thought about the way he had kissed her. So why the sudden chill? What was he afraid of? She walked into her room, switched on the light, then closed the door behind her. She crossed to the French doors, and pulled shut the drapes. But as she did, she caught a flicker of movement on the water.

Was someone out there? Not wanting to be seen, she turned off the light, then opened the doors and slipped onto the balcony.

Beneath the faint light of an antique lantern, the tall possum hunter she'd seen earlier stood on a flatboat, gliding across the glassy surface of the swamp. The red glow of a cigarette burned brightly between his lips. He turned toward her.

Laura stepped back into the dark shadows of the house. Could he see her? When he didn't turn away, she slid back into her room and locked the doors behind her. What was he doing out there? Possum hunting? The words ricocheted through her mind, but didn't dispel the unease spreading through her.

She stood still, the total darkness of the room pulsating around her.

"There's nothing here," she whispered. Nothing to be afraid of. Logically, she knew it was true and yet, her heart beat faster. Her palms dampened. She rubbed them across her jeans. She'd let that man spook her. She needed to toughen up or she wouldn't last a week in this house.

She pulled on the drapes, parting them slightly. A shaft of moonlight sliced through the room. She changed into thin cotton shorts and a T-shirt and slid beneath the covers.

"Nothing here," she muttered again, and as her head hit the pillow, fatigue fell over her like a heavy cloak.

Maybe Drew was right. Maybe she should put the past behind her and go home. She pictured his green eyes and felt a small catch in her chest. She thought of his voice, deep and sultry with the slightest twang of a Louisiana accent, and his hands—soft, gentle, hungry.

He had kissed her like a man starving for her touch. They'd clung to each other as if they were the only two people left in the world. He wanted her as much as she wanted him. She knew it. Kisses don't lie. So why had he pushed her away?

She fell asleep, thinking about his lips, his tongue. And the way his warm hands might feel tangled in her hair, moving down her neck, making a slow perusal of her collarbone. He'd linger on her breasts, circling, measuring their weight and absorbing their softness before moving down her belly and…

Laura's eyes flew open. It was still dark. How long had she been asleep? Then she felt it—a slight lift of the sheets, a flutter of movement at the foot of the bed. She shifted, her body tensing. A sinewy smoothness moved against her foot...her knee...up her thigh.

A high-pitched scream burst like fire through her fear-tightened chest. She pulled her knees up then rolled out of the bed. Her feet catching on the blankets, she tumbled onto the floor, landing hard on the area rug. She reached upward, groping for the lamp on the bedside table. Her arm brushed against something and it crashed to the floor, shattering.

She scurried backward away from the bed. Someone pounded on the door. She jumped, but couldn't see anything in the dark.

"Laura!" The door burst open. Light filled the room. Drew stood bare-chested and clad only in boxer shorts. "What is it? What happened?"

Laura turned to the bed and the tangle of blankets pulled halfway to the floor. She gasped a breath then looked around the lighted room. Nothing—no one there. Had she had another one of her nightmares?

Heat crept up her cheeks.

"Laura, speak to me." Drew's voice softened.

She stood, bracing herself against the wall then took a step toward him.

"Watch out for the glass," he warned, and stooped to pick up the large shards from a broken vase.

She inhaled a deep steadying breath and finally found her voice. "There's something in my bed."

They both looked at bed. It didn't look as though

there was anything there. But she'd felt it. She hadn't been dreaming.

Had she?

Drew walked toward the bed, careful not to step on the splintered glass.

"Under the covers," she said, her voice sounding strained. A shiver coursed through her as she remembered the feel of it against her leg. It was probably a giant bug, the kind that only lives in deep, dark, ugly swamps.

Drew pulled back the blankets

Laura cringed and squeezed both eyes shut. Slowly, she opened them, squinting.

Nothing was there.

"Check under the pillow," she urged. Were her nightmares back? Had she dreamed the whole thing?

Drew lifted the pillow.

Laura stared in disbelief at a small silk beaded bag. "What is it?"

"A gris-gris.

"A what-what?" Her throat tightened as a chill moved through her, seeping into her bones.

"Voodoo."

"Why would someone put that...thing under my pillow?"

"I don't know, but I promise you, I'll find out." He took the object off her bed and placed it on the bedside table.

"Still that's not what I felt. It was down by my feet...my thigh." Her voice splintered over the word.

He yanked the covers toward him with so much force the bed shifted a few inches away from the wall. Moving fast, a black snake at least five feet long slithered out from under the bed.

Laura screamed and jumped up onto the bed, squealing as shivers of revulsion surged through her.

Drew lunged for the French doors, throwing them open wide. The snake whipped out the doors and onto the balcony and through the rails. Drew slammed the doors shut and bolted the lock. "I hate snakes."

Laura couldn't move.

"There, it's gone."

"It was in my bed. With me!" she reiterated, in case he didn't grasp the scope of her meaning. Shudders coursed through her, growing stronger with each passing thought of how that thing had felt sliding against her skin.

"This room hasn't been used for a while. It could have been in here for months. From what I've heard, it was a cold winter. I'm sure it was looking for warmth," Drew offered.

"That's not comforting. Besides, I slept here last night. Are you saying that thing could have been in bed with me all night?" Her voice sounded shrill as anxiety crawled across her skin.

He took a step toward her. "It's okay now. It's gone."

She felt something brush against her hand and lurched back.

Drew took her hand and rubbed it. "Come on now, step down off the bed. How about we go downstairs for a hot cup of tea."

She shook her head. She didn't want tea. She didn't want sleep. She didn't want anything.

"Okay, then let's get you back in bed."

She jerked away from him, her vision snapping back into focus. "No way."

"The snake's gone. I promise."

"I don't care. I'm never sleeping in that bed again."

A smile hovered at the corners of his lips. "All right. Then you can sleep in my bed."

She stared at him, standing before her practically naked. A fine specimen of golden-bronzed skin and rippling muscles defined to mouthwatering perfection. Damn, he looked good. And at any other time, she would love to take him up on his offer.

For a distracting second, she let her mind go there, imagining what it, what he, would feel like. Her gaze moved over his body, and she itched to run her fingers along the strong lines of his biceps, to feel his skin next to hers.

Oh yeah. She couldn't say the thought didn't appeal to her, just a little.

"I'll sleep in here," he added.

She sighed in frustration and looked around the room—at the shards of broken glass, at the gris-gris thing, whatever it was, lying on her nightstand and at her mother's small rag doll sitting on the dresser. She crinkled her brow. Was that where she'd left it?

"No," she muttered.

"What?"

"I—I don't want to be alone."

He helped her down from the bed away from the glass, then out into the hall to his room. He stopped outside the doorway. "There are no voodoo trinkets or snakes in here, I promise."

She followed him into his room.

He pulled up the rumpled covers on his bed so she could see beneath them. "See? All clear."

Laura forced a smile.

He turned toward the door.

"Drew."

He hesitated.

"Will you lie down with me? Just for a little while? Just until I fall asleep?" With her pride lodged in her throat, she waited for his answer.

Reluctance filled his eyes. Then as his gaze took in her tight T-shirt and thin shorts, they darkened with something else. Longing?

"Please?" she added. "I don't want to be alone."

He nodded.

Relieved, she climbed into his bed. She could still

feel the warmth from his body lingering on the sheets. He lay next to her, their bodies barely touching.

"Thank you," she whispered.

"You're welcome."

For the first time all day she felt completely safe. The only thing that could possibly make this moment better would be if he pulled her close and pressed his lips against hers.

She took a deep breath, inhaling his clean male scent into her. If it weren't for him, she wouldn't be able to stay another day in this house. Certainly not another night.

Why had someone put that gris-gris thing under her pillow? What was it for? She thought of the hunter outside her window, of the snake in her bed.

"Someone definitely doesn't want me here," she whispered.

Under the covers he took her hand and lifted it to his lips. He placed a gentle kiss across her knuckles and stared into her eyes. "Whatever happened to your mother, you can't risk staying here. Not anymore."

She thought of the car almost hitting her in the street. Maybe it hadn't been an accident as Jeanne had claimed. And she still didn't know who made that strange phone call. Her mother obviously wasn't here and hadn't been for a long time. That person lied to bring her here. Why? Why would anyone care enough to go to all that trouble? They wouldn't.

No one ever had.

She pushed the thought away.

"I've lived my whole life fighting the fact that I was abandoned, that I wasn't worth coming back for. I need to know the truth before I can move forward and put the past behind me. I want to build a life full of people I will let close to me because I'll no longer fear they'll walk out and leave me. I can't do that until I know why my mom left me. That's why I can't go. Not yet."

Something flashed in his eyes, but it was too dark to gauge his reaction. As the silence stretched between them, she realized she'd been foolish to open up a vein and let loose her deepest fears. She'd exposed herself like an idiot. She waited with held breath for him to say something—anything.

But he didn't.

Maybe he was the one who'd been messing with her mind. He knew how much voodoo gave her the willies. Did he want her to go so badly he'd plant a gris-gris under her pillow to scare her into leaving? Was that how the snake had gotten up two stories and into her bed?

No! Her mind protested, but not loudly enough to completely quell the nagging doubts.

Chapter 8

Drew woke slowly with a smile on his face and a burning stiffness in his groin. The last vestiges of his dream drifted from his mind—thick black hair and sweet luscious lips.

Laura.

She was sensuous and beautiful with a unique combination of strength and vulnerability that spoke to him like no other.

He couldn't have her. She was marked by death. He shifted trying to find a more comfortable position, but his erection was rock-hard and the only relief he'd find for that was in Laura's arms.

Something soft and supple moved against him. Laura's sweet smell filled him. Drew's eyes shot open.

Laura's thigh brushed his. Had she been rubbing up against him all night? No wonder he'd awakened with a blazing fire burning through him. He'd meant to move into her room after she'd fallen asleep, but he'd drifted off, too.

The early-morning light played across Laura's face. She was even more beautiful while sleeping. He edged a little closer. A strand of her long hair tickled his chest. He longed to wake her with a kiss and see her gaze up at him with sleepy blue eyes. Temptation urged him, reminding him of the kiss they shared the day before. How she'd tasted and the soft little noises of pleasure she'd made.

A low guttural moan rumbled in his throat.

She rubbed against him once more, her silky skin against... *Damn!*

Desire throbbed within him. He needed distance or else he'd make love to her right then and there and damn the consequences. He swore under his breath and moved as far away from her as the bed would allow.

The only chance Laura had to survive would be if he could get her out of there, and that wouldn't happen if he took her into his bed and allowed her into his heart.

He wouldn't let himself grow that close only to lose her. He peered down at her long shapely leg. He couldn't have her. Not even for a second.

She rolled over, her lips parting as she blew out a soft breath.

Or a minute.

Her cotton shirt lifted, baring a smooth, taut belly.

An hour?

He swore and got out of bed. Taking a change of clothes with him, he went into the bathroom to shower. He had a lot to do today. Productive things. Things that might help Laura find the answers she was looking for so that she could go back home. Things that didn't involve stealing kisses and making love until noon. No matter how badly he wanted to.

First, he'd start with his mother. He wanted to find out what she knew about all this voodoo crap and how she was involved in it. But even as he scrubbed his head and lathered his body, trying to formulate an agenda for the day, pale blue eyes kept needling him, along with the thought of soft lips moving beneath his.

Heat fired within him once more, shooting through his body. He turned the water to cold, letting the icy spray sluice over his skin for a long minute. Focus. Figure out what was going on around here.

Get your mind off sexing Laura and onto getting rid of her. He turned off the water and roughly rubbed his towel across his body. Someone brought Laura here under false pretenses. The fact that he was here at the same time was too big a coincidence to ignore.

Quickly he dressed then walked through the house and into the kitchen while rubbing his head dry with a towel.

"Good morning," his mother greeted from beside the stove.

"Still cooking?" he asked, slightly surprised to see her there so early, but thankful for the pot of coffee he smelled brewing and the opportunity to get some answers without Laura around to hear them.

"You betcha. I want everything to be perfect for your party."

He cringed at the reminder. "I'm a little old for birthday parties, Mom. I wish you wouldn't go to so much trouble."

Her Avon-red lips twitched. "Don't be ridiculous, it will be fun. Breakfast?"

"No, thanks. Just coffee."

Her expression twisted with disapproval. "How'd you sleep?"

"Great." He thought of Laura still lying in his bed and felt a slight thump in his chest. He liked the idea of her being there. He could almost pretend she was lying there waiting for him. Almost.

"Somehow a snake got into Laura's bed last night." He watched her expression searching for a hint of surprise or guilt.

She froze, her eyes widening, the coffeepot poised over his cup.

Surprise.

He let out a relieved breath. "She's okay. It wasn't poisonous. Just a mud snake."

"Sugar?" She resumed pouring his coffee.

He nodded and she put the sugar bowl in front of him.

"I found this under her pillow." He placed the gris-gris on the table.

She sighed. Definitely *guilt.*

He stirred the sugar into his cup and bit down on his annoyance. "What is it?"

"Just a spell to ease Laura's mind. She seemed so anxious. I thought it would be better for her if she didn't remember too much about what happened here all those years ago. And then after Jeanne called to tell me what had happened in town, well I was sure a little gris-gris spell was exactly what Laura needed to help her relax and get some sleep."

Drew stopped midsip, the coffee cup hovering next to his mouth as he stared at her in disbelief.

"I know you hate the voodoo. I'm sorry. I was only trying to help Laura."

"You haven't. In fact, she's totally wigged out by the whole voodoo thing."

"Is she?" His mother smiled, a condescending little grin that sparked a quiver of uneasiness in him. "There's no reason to be. You know that. Voodoo is harmless."

Is it? "Well, she's upset. So the next time you

want to help Laura sleep, stick with warm milk and cookies."

"I won't do it again. I promise." She gave his shoulder a little pat, then walked back to attend to whatever was in her pot on the stove.

Gris-gris, juju, voodoo spells. It had been a long time since Drew had given them any thought. Was it possible his mother was using a spell to block Laura's memories? Was there even such a thing? And was she using the same spell on him? Was that why he was having such a hard time remembering exactly what had happened the night Laura almost drowned? He studied his mother's face over the brim of his cup and was suddenly certain voodoo *was* dangerous.

Laura opened her eyes and stared at the empty pillow next to hers. She stretched and glanced around the room. She was alone. Relief mingled with a smidgen of disappointment filled her. She remembered waking up in the middle of the night and realizing Drew was still with her. She'd longed to wrap her arms around his chest and snuggle up next to him, but she couldn't figure out where she stood with him. One moment he was kissing her and the next he was pushing her away.

She got up and stepped out onto the balcony overlooking the swamp. The day outside was gorgeous. Sunlight glistened off the water. Colorful blossoms swayed in the breeze. Joyous birds frolicked in the trees. She took in a deep breath of fresh air and, for a second, could almost see the charm of living on the bayou.

Until she remembered the snake in her bed.

She turned, stepped back into the room and closed the doors behind her. She was anxious to get showered and dressed when she noticed a hand-written note with her name on it sitting on the bedside table.

Curious, she picked it up.

Laura,
I have some information about your mother. Meet me out back. Follow the path to the family cemetery. This will soon be over and you'll be able to go home. Pack your bags. I've booked you on a one o'clock flight.
Drew

Why did he want her to meet him at the cemetery? Was he implying that her mother was dead? Laura's chest tightened. She closed her eyes then shook her head. She didn't believe it. If her mother had been dead all these years and buried in the cemetery, Miss Martha would have known about it. She would have told her. This was a trick, a ruse to get her to stop searching and go back home.

Did Drew want her gone that badly?

Laura crumpled the note in her hand. How dare he make flight reservations for her? Could he make it any clearer he didn't want her here at this house… in *his* bed! Angry tears stung the back of her eyes. She blinked several times keeping them at bay.

She wasn't going anywhere. She would leave when she'd accomplished what she'd come here to do—find her mother! And after seeing all her mother's things, holding the doll she'd created, Laura wanted to find her more than ever.

She hurried down the hall to her room and stood in the doorway, hesitating for only a moment before pushing into the room. She took a quick shower and dressed. She'd see whatever it was that Drew wanted to show her, and then she'd make it crystal clear that she wasn't going to be on that flight.

She was only a small distance away from the house on the path toward the graveyard that she and Drew had taken only yesterday when she realized she was trudging through muck in thin canvas shoes.

She groaned as she stepped in a particularly wet spot. Her shoe made a terrible sucking noise as she pried it loose. She stepped cautiously through the underbrush that had grown over the path and thought of the snake in her bed. Boots. As soon as she went into town again, she'd buy herself a good pair of boots.

Her progress was slow and while earlier the morning had seemed bright and cheerful, now it grew daunting and gloomy as black clouds filled the sky.

Why hadn't Drew awakened her? Why the cryptic note? Because he's a coward.

But was he? She slowed and tried to clear her mind long enough to give her growing doubts credence. A bush next to her shook, its leaves rattling. Laura froze and eyed the plant. Nothing moved. After a moment, she wiped her damp hands on her jeans and continued cautiously forward, waiting for some creature to jump out at her any moment.

None appeared. Nothing gross and furry, nothing reptilian and slimy.

Nor did she see Drew.

Where was he?

"Drew!" she called, but he didn't answer. She rounded a bend in the path and stepped deeper into the shadows of a cypress tree, its branches dripping with Spanish moss. The smell of decay was strong here, reaching inside her with each breath. Tendrils of anxiety crawled across her skin. She'd been here before. The image of the tree with its cloying parasite pushed at the walls in her head, trying to break through.

She focused on the various relaxation techniques her doctor had taught her, trying to coax her memories to the surface, but it was no use. She kept hitting a black wall.

She stopped trying and continued to walk, letting the screeching cries of a bird fill her mind, the saturated soil's strong stench fill her nose, the bite of the breeze chill her face.

Was Drew even here? The thought heightened her apprehension. She peered into the smokelike haze thickening around her. Swamp mist rolled over her skin and into her mouth leaving her with a salty, almost musty taste.

She saw the cemetery's iron gates, almost hidden beneath veils of Spanish moss. The iron was thick and old and in places, rusted beyond repair. The rails rose six feet high and crested into sharp wicked points.

Her insides tightened. She should go back. This was stupid. Drew wasn't here. But instead of listening to the warning voice in her mind, she walked forward drawn by the desolate graveyard.

Through the gates several large tombs and mausoleums of every shape and size sat aboveground out of the water's corrosive reach. Some graves were quite elaborate, adorned with marble angels and pewter crosses, while others, the older ones, were just brick-and-mortar boxes.

Enticed by the tombs, Laura barely noticed the gate's protesting whine as she pushed through and walked inside. She never imagined there had been so many Larames and shuddered at the thought of one day ending up there herself.

She stopped before a mausoleum with Paul's name etched into the stone and placed her hand on the cool marble. She had a vague recollection of standing in this same spot as a child, of her mother squeezing her hand too tight, of red-rimmed eyes under a black veil.

Not the eyes of a woman who had killed her husband.

For a full minute Laura stood still, listening. But she didn't hear a sound. Not even from the birds. All was deathly silent. She shook off the insidious fear stirring within her and continued on, reading the names carved into the marble. She couldn't help wondering about those people's lives and how they'd died.

Lost in thought, she rounded a large mausoleum, her fingertips gliding across the cool marble's smooth surface, and stopped. The wooden flatboat with the old lantern dangling from a hooked pole sat in the water at the edge of the swamp not ten feet in front of her.

Empty.

Laura's stomach dropped.

"Hello, Delilah."

Her heart slammed against her chest at the sound of his raspy voice. Turning, she faced the possum hunter.

His rheumy gray gaze slid across her face. "You shouldn't've come back here. You're not welcome in the bayou."

"I'm not Delilah. I'm Laura Larame, Delilah's daughter."

He stepped closer to her. Sniffing the air.

She took a step back.

"Your kind of magic isn't wanted here."

"I don't know any magic."

"Tell that to my Georgette," he snarled through rotten teeth. "That poor child has never found her rest. She still wanders the swamp, looking for the witch that killed her. Looking for you."

Laura stiffened. Shudders cascaded down her spine. *Georgette?* The girl who died with Paul?

"We all know what you did, Delilah. You *will* pay for your sins." He stepped closer, close enough that she could smell the stench of death rolling off his skin.

Every instinct within her told her to turn and run, but instead she stood her ground. She would not be intimidated, bullied or scared off. By anyone. She straightened her shoulders and lifted her chin.

"As I said, my name is Laura, and I believe you are standing on Larame property. I suggest you leave."

Surprise widened his eyes. "Heed my warnings, girl. If you know what's good fer you, you'll turn tail and leave back to where you came from."

Girl? She cocked a brow. Maybe this man wasn't as delusional as he first appeared. He turned and stepped onto his boat, picked up his pole and pushed off, gliding away from her across the glassy water.

He passed what at first appeared to be a log floating between the leaves from a low-hanging branch, but in the bayou things weren't always what they seemed. Cold, unblinking eyes stared at her—an alligator searching for his morning meal.

Once the hunter was far enough away, Laura stepped forward and peered into the black murky water. His boat had been moored over a tomb that was completely swallowed by the swamp. She'd thought she saw something red moving beneath the surface.

She stepped forward to get a closer look. An egret landed on the water causing ripples to block her view. At least she hoped it was the bird that caused them. She took another step closer and leaned forward, peering into the dark waters.

Mud shifted beneath her feet. She sank into the muck. Swamp water covered her ankles. She tried to pull free, but the swamp had her, pulling her down.

Panicked, she raised her foot. It broke free, but the momentum knocked her off balance. Pinwheeling her arms, she tried to stay standing. *She could not fall into the grave-laden waters!* Horror seeped into her, sending her free-falling into uncontrolled terror.

Screaming, she lost her balance and fell forward. Her knees hit first. Her hands splashing into the mud. Her face dipping beneath the surface. She saw marble and brick, rippling within the sediment. Tombs!

And some kind of red fabric.

She pushed backward out of the water, and scrambled onto the muddy shore. She gulped a terrified breath and rubbed the swamp water from her face with the inside of her arm. Oh, God, she was covered in algae and mud and the decaying stench of the swamp.

"Dammit all to hell!" She pushed herself out of the muck and wove her way through the tombs back toward the gates. She was dripping and slimy and miserable. Before she reached the gates, she heard a noise behind her. Dread skittered up her stiffened spine.

"Laura?" Drew's voice came from behind her.

Fury mingled with relief and embarrassment formed a molten stew of emotion. She wheeled on him.

He stared at her for a long moment, his back straightening, his gaze turning hard as he took a step back away from her. "What are you doing out here?" he asked, through a tight jaw.

"Looking for you!" She bit her bottom lip, clamping down on her fury.

"Me?"

"Yes, and if you think I'm going to be on that flight this afternoon, you're sadly mistaken. I'm not going anywhere but back to the house to take a hot shower."

He stood still, his dark eyes watching her out of an expressionless face. She hated it when he looked at her like that. The coldness in his gaze reminded her that she didn't know anything about him.

In fact, the only thing she had discovered since

coming here was that someone seemed real determined to scare her into leaving and, so far, he and the hunter had been the only ones to come right out and tell her to go.

"What happened?" he asked.

"Obviously, I fell in the swamp."

"I've warned you—" He stopped midsentence and pushed his lips together so hard they whitened.

Warned her? A shiver tore through her that had nothing to do with her wet clothes.

He turned and headed back down the path toward the house.

He wasn't getting away that easy. She fell into step beside him. "So what did you find out about my mother? What was so important that I had to meet you way out here?"

He stopped and turned to her, his cold, hard gaze locking onto hers. "What are you talking about?"

"You said to meet you here. I came. Where were you?"

His face contorted with confusion and suddenly she knew. Dismay widened her eyes and her throat went dry. "You didn't leave me a note, did you?"

Chapter 9

After a long hot shower, Laura finally got the rancid smell of the swamp off her. She ambled to her room in a towel in no hurry to face Drew again, to see the tightness of his jaw, the hard lines around his mouth, to wonder why he was doing his best to scare her into leaving.

She pulled open her underwear drawer and reached inside, but instead of cotton, her hand brushed across burlap and twine. Gripping the edge of the dresser, she leaned forward and peered inside, grabbed the object and pulled it out of the drawer.

A voodoo doll with large black empty eye sockets sunk deep into a white skull was clutched in her hand. Disgusted, she flung the doll. It rolled across the top of the dresser, then came to a stop, lying on its side, facing her.

Several strands of long shiny back hair flowed out the top of the head—hair that looked a lot like hers. Hand trembling, she reached for the doll, her fingertips hovering over the strands as she forced herself to feel the hair.

Was it real? *It felt real.* She yanked her hand back then noticed a child's necklace wrapped several times around the doll's neck. A small unicorn pendant dangled, sparkling in the light. She'd been wearing one like it in one of her mother's photos on the wall in the hallway.

Was the necklace hers?

Was the hair?

Repulsed, she turned away from the doll. Drew stood in the doorway watching her.

"Did you put it there?" she demanded, pulling the towel tighter around her.

"What?" His gaze raked her face then moved beyond her.

"It was in my drawer…my *underwear* drawer." An uncontrollable shiver shook her.

Drew crossed the room, picked up the doll and examined it, his fingers brushing across green feathers attached to its back.

Fear seeped like ice-cold water through her veins to painfully tighten her chest. "Did you put some kind of creepy voodoo spell on me?"

"No. Someone is trying to scare you, but it's not me." His green eyes locked onto hers. "I'll find out who's behind this."

She wished she could believe him. She wanted to believe him, to trust him. But what if it was him toying with her emotions, and trying to chase her away? He seemed the most logical suspect. He had easy access to her thoughts, her fears...her *room*. But she couldn't reconcile her suspicions with the way he made her feel last night—safe, secure, *wanted.*

As she looked at him, she realized it didn't matter how he made her feel, she had to stay strong and not let whoever was behind this mess spook her.

Drew touched her arm, the soft gesture comforting, even as she tried to ignore it.

"I promise, Laura, if you let me, I'll do everything I can to keep you safe." There was a slight catch in his voice, a hesitancy that spoke of his sincerity.

She wanted to believe him. Oh, how she wanted to trust that he truly did care about her and wasn't just turning her into a sappy fool.

"Tell me about this morning," he said. "About the note. Where did you find it?"

Apprehension prickled her spine. "On the table next to your bed. If you didn't leave the note, then someone must have come in while we were sleeping and put it there."

She wasn't sure which sounded worse.

"And I can assure you, this wasn't there yesterday." She gestured toward the voodoo doll.

"My mother admitted to placing the gris-gris bag under your pillow last night. She—"

"Your mother?"

"Yes, I'm sorry. She said she was only trying to help."

"Miss Martha practices voodoo?" As she said the words aloud something snapped in her mind, some hidden knowledge that made her at once panicked and sick.

She turned away from him, not sure where she should go or what she should do and leaned against the wall to steady herself.

Drew's hand lingered on her bare shoulder, his touch sending tingles down her back.

"She said it was only a spell to help you sleep, to keep you from remembering."

She looked at him over her shoulder. "Remembering?"

"Whatever happened the night your mom disappeared and you and I almost drowned in the swamp."

"How much do you remember of that night?" she asked.

His eyes shifted and he looked away.

She blew out an exasperated breath.

"Why would someone want you to go to the graveyard? Did you see anyone?"

She grimaced. "Yes. That strange man we saw on our way into town yesterday. The possum hunter. He was outside my bedroom last night on that weird boat of his, too."

"Did he say anything to you? Do anything?"

Uneasiness slid through her as she replayed the conversation. "He called me Delilah and told me to leave."

Drew sighed. "What does an old derelict have to do with any of this?"

"He said something about wanting justice for Georgette, but mostly I think he was trying to scare me. When I stood up to him, he called me a little girl. I don't think he would have referred to my mother, the voodoo priestess the locals seem to be so afraid of, as a little girl. He knew exactly who I was and what he was saying."

She leaned her head back against the wall and closed her eyes. Maybe she should go home.

"Are you going to be okay?" His voice was gentle, caressing.

Manipulative?

Her gaze perused his face, trying to figure him out.

"You can trust me," he said. "I know it's crazy, but I want to take care of you. I want to help you. I want..."

His eyes moving down her body...lingering. She became acutely aware that she was wearing only a towel. Awareness shot through her, sending a flush of heat up her chest. She shifted, the towel's cotton rubbing against her sensitive skin—across her back, her thighs, her bottom. Her tongue slipped out and she ran it across her lips.

His gaze followed the movement, and suddenly her nerve endings were chafing and sparking. His eyes caught hers.

"I want to believe you." She fought to keep herself from reaching for him. It seemed that no matter how strong her fears and doubts might be, she wanted him to touch her, to hold her tight. She wanted to feel more of those tingles...*everywhere*.

He placed his hand on the wall next to hers and moved one finger across hers. A simple gesture with miniscule contact and yet heat fired straight through her.

She really had no reason to distrust him. Since she first saw him standing in the front doorway, he'd only been kind and helpful. And incredibly sexy.

Hadn't he?

Her gaze flickered across his chest, over toned muscles under his thin shirt. She longed to run her fingers across them, stroking, caressing.

He'd been there for her when that car almost ran her down and again last night with the snake. If she truly believed that he had written that note, that she couldn't trust him, then would her body be responding so strongly to him?

"Swear to me you didn't write that note," she demanded.

"I swear," he said, his voice sounding raspy with caged desire.

And though she knew it was crazy, that she was operating on pure emotion, she believed him.

She *wanted* to believe him.

She wanted him.

I should leave. Right now. Turn around. Get out. But he didn't. Like a glutton for punishment, Drew stood there. His gaze dropped to her mouth. He sucked in a breath and the fruity smell of her shampoo filled him. She stood so close he could feel heat rolling off her. She was on edge, pumped up and looking even more beautiful with desire glistening in her eyes.

He wanted her. And worse, she wanted him. The sexual tension bouncing between them was palpable.

Mon Dieu. Surrendering to the fire, he seized her shoulders, pulling her to him and crushing her lips beneath his. He kissed her, long and hard, until he lost himself in her softness and the sweet taste of her mouth. He swam in the sensations until he was drowning.

A soft moan escaped her and he clung to the sound, as he would a raft in a turbulent sea. No! He couldn't do this. He steadied himself, released her and gulped a deep breath.

"Drew," Laura whispered, caressing her swollen lips with the tips of two fingers. "Tell me you want me."

Damn! How could he not want her?

She leaned into him, her gentle touch moving across his chest. He ached to remove his shirt, to feel her skin against his.

She nibbled the corner of his mouth, raining kisses along his jaw. His blood rushed through his system, heating his body temperature and fine-tuning his senses so that every touch, every breath left him aching for more.

"Oh, I want you," he said, his voice hoarse with unbridled passion. "And, I want you in my room, in my bed."

"Then show me." Her eyelids lowered. She gave her towel a tug and let it fell to the floor.

As if sucker punched, Drew inhaled sharply. Her breasts were incredible, larger then he'd expected and yet high and firm. The rosy tips of her nipples hardened under his perusal, showing him how much she wanted him to touch her there.

Oh, and how he wanted to touch them, to lick and suck them, but he hesitated. If he crossed this line, there would be no going back. No keeping her at bay. No keeping his emotions and desires in check.

And yet, he couldn't tear his gaze away. Her chest

rose and fell in short little gasps. She wanted him. He could see it in the intensity of her gaze, feel it in the warmth of her skin.

"I want to. You know I want to," he said, grasping onto his reason even as he felt himself slipping, felt all coherent thought washing away in a flood of desire.

He couldn't have her. He couldn't give up control. He had to go. Instead, he leaned forward, avoiding contact with her body and kissed her softly, his lips hovering over hers.

In an intimate caress, she ran the tip of her tongue across his mouth. His heart raced. Chills burst through his pores. Their tongues barely touched and yet, with that slight contact, he knew he had to have her.

There was no stopping. No going back. Softly, he touched her nipples, first one then the other. They hardened as he teased them with featherlight strokes while mimicking the soft play of their tongues. She let out a breathy moan, and it was all he could do not to lift her up into his arms right then and bury his stiff erection within her.

The image played across his mind and he thrust his tongue in and out of her mouth. His cock throbbed. He intensified their kiss, tangling his hand through her wet hair, pulling her closer to him, pressing his mouth hard against hers.

"Laura, are you sure?"

Please be sure.

Her hands slid up his chest to his shoulders, where she kneaded the taut muscles. She had strong, sure hands. And what he wouldn't give to feel those hands touching him...*all over.*

Her sweet lips moved across his collarbone, his shoulder, his throat, heating him to the boiling point. "I'm not sure of anything."

She moved her hands down his stomach. His breathing went shallow and his eyelids lowered. He had to take back control or she'd have him making love to her on the floor before they even got to the bed.

Her fingers wrestled with his belt, loosening it and unclasping his pants. "Not even you."

His pants fell to the ground to puddle around his shoes.

White heat fired through him. He slipped his hands down the curve of her waist then he picked her up. He carried her to the bed, kicking shut the bedroom door. He set her down and leaned over her, one hand braced on either side of her. This was it. The time for doubt had passed. He was way beyond the point of reason.

She smiled at him, then crooked her finger in a come-hither gesture.

His blood pulsed through him. She slipped her tongue into his mouth, rubbing it against his. Tasting him. Sparring with him.

He pulled her closer, capturing her tongue with

his, pressing his mouth hard against hers. She gave a small whimper of pleasure that shot straight through him. His hunger built. His tongue delved. She sucked on it, drawing it deeper.

They rolled on their sides, and he ran his hands down her slim back and shifted, pulling her beneath him. She bucked her hips, drawing him down into the juncture between her thighs. He nestled there. Feeling her warmth cradling him, the tickle of her hair stroking his sensitized skin.

She laced her fingers around his neck and pushed herself against him so he could feel every delicious curve.

He dipped his head and drew the rose-colored tip of her breast into his mouth, gently at first, then harder, sucking her nipple to a fine point.

She groaned, throwing her head back, moaning her pleasure, pressing her hips against him. She wanted him. He felt it in her touch, heard it in her throaty moans, smelled it in the sweet musk filling the air.

Blood thundered through his veins. He slipped his hand down her belly, his fingers playing with her soft curly hair, sliding inside the warm core of her. She was hot and very ready for him.

She grabbed hold of him, squeezing, stroking, her strong grip guiding him. He gasped at her touch and positioned himself above her. She smiled and he slid deep inside her. She arched, lifting her legs, cradling him within her moist, snug heat.

He began to move. Slowly at first, rocking back and forth, feeling each tingling sensation up and down the length of him. And the more he moved, the faster he moved, the deeper he wanted to go.

Her throaty moans urged him faster. Their movements were almost animalistic as they clutched each other.

He lost himself in the sensations pulsing through him, in the pale blue abyss of her desire-laden gaze, in her musky scent.

He could feel her heart racing, her blood pounding. Her grasp on his shoulders tightened and he knew there was nowhere else he wanted to be. With a surge of conviction, his passion crested.

He looked down at her and, for a split second, she expanded, bursting into an explosion of bright shimmering lights. He squinted, blocking out the intensity. She was a vision of white twinkling lights—a warm glow that reached inside him and filled him with such happiness his heart couldn't contain it.

She smiled, the lights almost starlike, swirling round and round each other, yet still keeping her form. Her pleasured scream shattered the vision. And she was Laura again, lying beneath him, her body pulsing around him, breaking his control and sending him tumbling over the edge of passion where he couldn't see, he couldn't think, he could only feel.

Chapter 10

Laura wasn't looking forward to this confrontation. But she had to know the truth about what Drew's mother was up to. Was she the one who left the voodoo doll in her room? No more games. While Drew was in the shower, she'd talk to Martha and demand the truth.

Laura walked into the kitchen.

"It's almost the big awakening," Martha said; her smile a little too wide, a little too bright. Candles of different shapes and sizes littered the room. She picked up a medium-size aluminum pot and poured hot wax into square tin cylinders with geometric designs beat into the sides. Next, she picked up a small bottle and squeezed a drop of liquid into the hot wax. A strange sour odor filled the room. It smelled familiar, but Laura couldn't quite place it.

"Martha, I found this next to the bed this morning. Do you recognize the handwriting?" She passed the crumpled note to Martha.

Martha read the note then handed it back to her. "I don't know. It says it's from Drew. Why, was there a problem?"

"What about this?" She placed the voodoo doll on the table.

Martha's eyes widened with surprise. "Oh, my. Where did you find that?"

"In my drawer. Do you know what it is?"

"Well, obviously it's a voodoo doll, though I must say it is an ugly little thing." She picked up the trash can and carried it over to her. "Here, throw it away."

Laura was tempted, but stopped herself. "No, I think I'll hold on to it for a little while longer."

"What on earth for?"

"Because if someone is coming into our rooms leaving these kinds of…gifts, then we need to know who it is and what they want."

Martha's gaze narrowed and her red lips thinned, but she didn't say a word, only turned back to the wax heating on the stove.

"Martha, Drew told me about the gris-gris," Laura continued, undeterred. "Are you sure there isn't anything you want to tell me about all this?"

Martha didn't turn or respond.

"Martha?"

She sighed, then slowly turned toward her. "I don't know what to say, Laura. I can't imagine why Drew is so determined to be inhospitable. I'm sorry for that, I really am. I'll have a talk with him."

Shocked, Laura stared at the woman who'd babysat her as a child. Who had always been wonderful to her. Could she be right? Did she just make mind shattering love to a man who was playing games with her? Lying to her?

Trepidation skittered along her nerves. "Martha, is there a key to my room? I'd like to start locking the door."

Martha tilted her head in sympathy. "If there was a key, it's been long lost. We've never had a reason for locks and keys way out here."

"Well, that may have been true, but I believe there is a reason now." She gestured toward the doll. "And not only that, there's some crazy hunter floating around on his boat at night, right out there." Laura pointed out the window toward the swamp. "It could very well have been him who put a snake in my bed and left me that doll."

And not Drew.

As soon as she had the thought, Drew walked into the room. Laura's heart skipped a beat.

"You mean Charlie Wallis?" Martha asked.

"That old derelict is Mabel's husband? What

happened to him?" Drew asked, his eyes finding Laura's.

"The poor man lost his mind after his daughter, Georgette, died," Martha said. "He's a harmless old fool, just glides around on his boat muttering about witches and ghosts and how the swamp speaks to him."

"What makes you so sure he's harmless?" Laura thought of the man's rusty hatchet. He hadn't appeared too harmless to her.

Martha's lips twisted into a smirk. "Oh, Charlie wouldn't hurt a soul."

"Tell that to the rodents," Laura muttered and stepped closer to Drew. Was it possible it had been him all along? The note, the doll, the snake?

"Martha, if you can find the keys to the bedroom doors, I would appreciate it."

Martha stared at her for a moment, her gaze shifting back and forth between her and Drew, then suddenly she smiled and wiped her hands on her apron.

"Of course. Whatever you need. I'm really sorry about all this nonsense, Laura." Martha gestured toward the voodoo doll still sitting on the table. "I hope you won't let it scare you away. You belong here at Lionsheart. It is and always will be your home. If you want the locks changed, I'll be happy to call Tom's Locksmith and take care of it for you first thing tomorrow. I want you to feel safe here. I'd do it today, but I have somewhere I need to be soon, so I'm sorry if I've been a little distracted."

Laura's shoulders dropped as the tension seeped out of her. "Thank you, Martha. That's very sweet of you. And yes, tomorrow would be great."

"We're going into town," Drew suddenly announced and picked up the doll off the table then took Laura's hand.

For a second, Laura hesitated. But she had to be smart if she was going to figure out the truth of what was going on. She had to determine who was the real Drew. The man who made incredible love to her? Or a man capable of doing anything to get her to leave this house.

Her house.

"You will be back for dinner, won't you? I'm trying out a new recipe I want to serve at the party and I want to make sure I have it just right," Martha said.

"I'm sure it will be fine," Drew said. "And yes, we'll be home for dinner," he added when she opened her mouth to protest.

She smiled and picked up another block of wax and added it to her pot. "Good. I'll see you then. And, Laura, you should get a sweater. There's a big storm coming in."

"Thanks, Martha."

In the foyer, Drew took a couple of umbrellas out of the canister by the front door as Laura hurried up the stairs to her room to get a sweater. She didn't doubt a storm was coming, a bad one.

And she had a feeling they could expect a lot more than rain.

Laura tried to calm the anxiety rumbling through her as they crossed the Devil's Walk Bridge. But they were going to Voodoo Mystique, and no matter how many times she tried to tell herself that it was only a store, the apprehension building within her told her that this voodoo store was much more than it appeared.

"What's Mary's story?" Laura asked as Drew drove them toward town.

He turned to her, his eyebrows raised. "What do you mean?"

"Maybe I was imagining it, but yesterday it seemed as if she was lurking in the shadows. Are you sure she'll want to see us?"

"Mary can be odd." Drew flipped on the windshield wipers as the storm's first raindrops bounced off the glass. "People thought she was in cahoots with your mother to kill Paul. She took a lot of flack after Paul's death, so I'm sure she doesn't feel that comfortable around the Larames."

"More voodoo stuff?"

Drew nodded. "She and your mother made Voodoo Mystique into *the* place for the occult outside New Orleans."

The storm broke loose as Drew parked the car. They sat for a moment watching the rain pummel the sidewalk and listening to it batter the roof of the car. The fury of the storm made their small space inside of the warm, dry vehicle seem all the more intimate.

Cozy, even. But it wasn't.

"Your mom denied leaving the doll in my drawer. In fact, she wanted to throw it away. Why would someone who practices voodoo react like that?"

He shook his head. "I don't know. My mother isn't always who she seems."

Laura stared at him. "She isn't the only one."

His brow crinkled with confusion, then his eyes softened and he reached out and touched her cheek. "You sure you're okay with going in the shop? I can handle this alone, if you want."

She fought a strong urge to let him do just that. But she had to talk to Mary for herself. She peered out the blurry windshield at the variety of voodoo dolls displayed in the window of the shop, and stifled a shiver. "I'll be fine. Mary was my mother's closest friend and business partner. I have to talk to her. I just hope she will have some answers for me."

He gave her hand a reassuring squeeze, and she was thankful he was there with her. Even if she couldn't fully trust him.

"Then let's do it," he said, handed her an umbrella and got out of the car.

It only took a cold, shocked breath for Laura to

realize her mistake in bothering with the umbrella. The wind and rain blew so hard she was drenched by the time she reached the storefront.

Together, they burst through the door in conjunction with thunder booming across the sky.

As they closed the door behind them, Mary's teacup rattled in the saucer. She leaned back in her chair in the front corner of the room silently studying them as they closed their umbrellas and left them by the door.

"I was wondering how long it would be before you came back for answers." She flipped over a card from the deck of tarot sitting in front of her.

Laura's stomach twisted as she tried to ignore the snap the heavy cards made as Mary flicked them.

With a gentle hand on her back, Drew led Laura to the small round table by the window where Mary sat. He pulled out a chair for Laura then grabbed the other for himself. "Thanks for seeing us," he said.

Laura quickly averted her eyes and looked out the window so she wouldn't have to see the grotesque and misshapen figures of the voodoo dolls surrounding her or the cards with their disturbing images spread out across the table.

"We have questions," Drew said. "But we were hoping you could help us with something else."

Laura turned to Mary and saw curiosity mingled with wariness fill her jet-black eyes.

So many secrets and lies.

And no one to trust.

"What do you need?" Mary said, scooping the cards into a pile. She wrapped the deck inside a swatch of purple silk and placed it inside an intricate wooden box.

Laura took several deep breaths and tried to relax, but found herself mesmerized by Mary's silver earrings peeking in and out from around her long black tresses.

Drew pulled the voodoo doll out of his pocket and laid it on the table. Laura watched Mary closely, noticing that the woman didn't touch the doll, not even to turn it around for a closer look.

"Is this one of the dolls you sell here?" Drew glanced around the shop as if seeking the answer.

Laura didn't have to ask. She remembered everything she'd seen the last time she was here—the dolls; the severed reptile heads; skulls of every shape, size and species and the snake skins.

She shuddered.

"No, it isn't," Mary said, still not touching the doll.

Laura could swear the woman paled slightly.

"You have so many. Are you sure?" Drew pushed.

Mary murmured something in response, but Laura was no longer listening.

The sensation of being watched prickled over her. The gloom thickened in the room. Rain clattered on the roof above them, but didn't offer the same intimacy as it had in the car. Instead it sounded like the barrage from a thousand angry gods. Lightning arced, filling the room with an eerie blue glow.

Laura darted a glance out the window, afraid of what she'd see. Nothing. There was no one there. She lifted her shoulders against the wisp of cold curling around her neck and covertly looked behind her.

No one.

No one else was in the store. There wasn't anyone watching her, except the hundreds of black holes staring from the skulls of the voodoo dolls.

But she felt it. Felt eyes boring into her soul. Her stomach churned.

"Are there any other voodoo shops around where someone could have purchased this doll?" Drew persisted.

Mary shook her head and stood abruptly. "Would you all like some hot tea?"

Drew sat back in his chair. "That would be nice, thanks."

Laura watched her disappear through a back door. "She knows something. She wouldn't even go near the doll."

He reached for her hand. His touch was warm and gentle, and reminded her of earlier when he'd held her in his arms. She wanted that now. Wanted to get out of this shop, forget all her fears and doubts and just be with him.

But what if he had left her the note? The doll? She peered into his eyes hoping to glean the truth from him.

"Don't worry. We'll get her to tell us what she knows." He leaned forward and lightly touched his lips to hers.

"How is it that you happened to be home visiting at the exact time I needed you?"

He smiled, though for some reason it didn't quite reach his eyes. "You can't fight destiny."

Or coincidence? If there was such a thing.

He brought her hand to his lips and gently kissed her closed fingers. The tension seeped out of her shoulders and, for a moment, as she stared into his warm gaze, she was certain he wouldn't do anything to hurt her.

But only for a moment.

"So, where did you find the doll?" Mary returned to the room carrying a tray holding a bright copper kettle, a sugar bowl and two more teacups.

"Someone left it for me in my underwear drawer," Laura answered.

Mary's lips pursed, but she didn't say a word as she set the teacups on the table and poured hot tea into them.

Laura wrapped her hands around a cup, letting the warmth fill her. "I believe that necklace—" she pointed to the unicorn wrapped tightly around the doll's neck "—was one I wore as a child. And the hair..."

She touched her own hair. "It could be mine." A chill that had nothing to do with the weather moved through her.

Mary's brow creased as she frowned, but she didn't say a word.

Why wouldn't she tell them what they needed to know? Frustration filled Laura as the strong scent of sandalwood incense made her head begin to throb.

"You must know something about this doll. Something you're not sharing with us."

Mary sat back in her chair and studied Laura for a moment, her eyes narrowing in contemplation.

"Are you sure you've never seen this doll?" Laura persisted.

"I never said I hadn't seen it." Mary took a long sip of her tea, her black gaze holding Laura's over the rim of the cup. "I said I hadn't sold it."

Laura stiffened in her chair, irritation stealing the last of her patience. "You recognize the doll, then? Do you know who made it? Or why someone would put my old jewelry on it and leave it in my drawer?"

"It's an *Enemy Be Gone* doll," Mary said softly, her voice nearly drowned out by the clatter of the rain on the roof.

Laura leaned forward, determined to hear it all, no matter how much it sickened her. "What is it for?"

"It's a doll created to make someone leave. To get rid of someone's presence."

Laura stole a glance at Drew, but if she was hoping for some sort of reaction she was disappointed. He had that same cold impassive look she was beginning to recognize.

"It's also a ceremonial doll used to aid the spirits in finding the chosen one."

The whisper of cold that had brushed Laura's neck turned into clutching, icy fingers. "What is the chosen one?" Just saying the words nearly choked her.

"The one marked to leave."

The tight band of fear wrapped around Laura's heart, squeezed. Why did everyone want to get rid of her?

"Who would leave me this thing?"

Mary shrugged, but her nonchalant body language didn't match the alarm growing in her eyes. "You must be careful, Laura. Staying at Lionsheart might not be the safest choice for you. The Inn across the street is where you should be."

Another warning? Laura's gaze met Drew's, then she turned back and leaned forward, placing both palms flat on the table, her eyes locking on Mary's. "If you know something about all this, about everything that's been happening to me, you would tell me, wouldn't you?"

"Because I was your mother's best friend?"

"I hope that counts for something."

Mary fiddled with her cup for a long moment. "I can tell you that this doll wasn't bought in any store."

"How do you know?" Drew asked.

"It was handmade. By someone here in town. Someone familiar with the...arts."

Drew's voice turned cold. "Are you saying that my mother made this?"

Laura thought of the gris-gris bag Drew said Martha had left for her, and the altar in the attic. Was it possible it had been Martha all along? And if so, why did she purposely make Laura think it had been Drew?

"Not your mother," Mary said, her voice deepening. Her gaze focused on Laura. "Hers."

The word shot straight through Laura with laser precision. She jumped out of the chair turning her back on Mary. Then she remembered all the dolls in the attic. Many had been faceless and unfinished. She put two and two together then fell back into her chair almost defeated by the realization. "My mother made voodoo dolls?"

Drew handed her a filled teacup, obviously trying to calm her nerves. She took it, then put it down and fixed her eyes on Mary. "Why?"

"It was quite lucrative and she was very good at it," Mary said. "She also made dolls for children, small rag dolls sold at exclusive toy shops in New Orleans." She sighed. "Unfortunately those didn't sell as well.

We formulated a plan and created Voodoo Mystique never dreaming it would work so well. Nor had we realized how dire the consequences would be."

"That's when Delilah reinvented herself as a voodoo priestess?" Drew asked.

"Exactly, so we could sell more dolls." Mary's face turned solemn.

"But why?" Laura asked. "My mother was married to a Larame. What could she have possibly needed money for that she would go to such extreme measures?"

"Your mother and Paul were planning on leaving. Paul no longer wanted to work for his father's law firm. They didn't want to live at Lionsheart. They wanted to leave Louisiana and make a fresh start somewhere else."

Laura stared at her. Something didn't sound right about this. If they had wanted to go, why not just leave? Why the secrets? Unless...

"I'm sure Randal and Jeanne weren't too happy about that." Drew reached behind him and took a large candle off a nearby shelf.

Unless her parents were afraid of something, Laura finished her thought. Or someone. Had they been in danger?

"The Larames never found out," Mary said. "Delilah was close to having the money they needed, but then Paul's car went over the Devil's Walk Bridge and he died."

Drew kept turning the candle around in his hand, staring at it, smelling it. The candle looked a lot like the one Drew's mother had been making earlier. Did she make them for Mary to sell in this shop?

"Then you and Laura almost drowned. After that, Delilah disappeared, and no one has seen her since."

"What about that?" Laura asked. "How on earth did I end up in the swamp?"

"No one knows," Mary said and fiddled with pouring herself another cup of tea.

"What about Georgette? What did she have to do with anything?" Drew persisted.

"Wrong place, wrong time."

What was she hiding? A cold whisper of air touched Laura's cheek. She whipped her head around, but again, saw nothing. She shuddered and thought about how much she hated this creepy place.

Drew set the candle down and leaned back in his chair. "Are you sure that's all there was to it?"

"Of course. Why?"

"Mabel had an intense reaction to Laura. And Charlie...well, he's been hanging around a lot."

"Georgette was their only daughter. After her death their lives fell apart along with their marriage. Charlie gave up his job, his house, his family to become a drifter. They needed someone to blame. They settled on Delilah."

A silence stretched between them and Drew picked

up the candle again and held it to his nose. "What can you tell me about these candles?"

Her lips twisted into a frown. "Not much. They're used in ceremonies."

"Voodoo ceremonies?" Laura asked.

Mary nodded, confirming what Drew had said about Martha. If she didn't practice voodoo, why would her kitchen be filled with voodoo candles? Some of the tightness left Laura's chest as she looked at Drew. Martha had lied about him. But why?

"What is that I smell?" he asked, taking another whiff.

"Vinegar," Mary said.

His eyebrows rose with surprise before he set the candle back down.

"Mary, is my mother here?" Laura demanded. Maybe Martha lied about her mother, too.

"Excuse me?"

"Yesterday I was almost run down. Last night, I found a snake in my bed. Today, someone left that doll in my drawer. A doll you tell me my mother once made."

Mary stood and picked up the candle Drew had left on the table then walked past them and placed it back on the shelf. "True, but someone added the hair and the necklace. They had to have had those already. I'd say someone wants you gone pretty bad."

That wasn't an answer.

"Is there any chance that person is my mother?"

Laura persisted, knowing she sounded almost desperate. "Is there any chance that she's alive, and for some reason, she doesn't want me to find her?"

"No." Mary sat back down and stared at her, taking her measure, obviously trying to decide how much, if anything, to say.

"Why not? How can you be so sure? She could easily have had a lock of my hair and my old necklace."

Mary leaned forward. "For your mother, you always came first. She wouldn't have left you alone, if she'd had a choice. Never."

Laura replayed what Mary said over in her mind. They were the words she'd always hoped to hear and yet a deep sadness seeped through her, weakening her, as if it came right out of her bones. "Are you sure?" Her voice broke.

"Absolutely," Mary said. "I've never been surer of anything in my life. If your mother didn't come back for you, it was because she couldn't."

Her words reverberated through Laura's mind like the clank of a graveyard gate.

Because she couldn't.

A sharp pain twisted inside her. It was the truth. Deep in her heart, she'd always known it. "I guess I was just hoping..."

Mary rose from her chair. "Your mother was very special to me. She loved you so much. Someone stopped her from coming to you, and now someone's leaving you warnings. Don't take them lightly, Laura. Go home. Go back to San Francisco before it's too late. There's nothing more for you to do here, and nothing to stay for. The past is gone."

Mary's words destroyed all hope in Laura's heart.

Her mother had to be dead.

Mary pulled a chain from around her neck and held it out to Laura. "This is something you might want."

Laura stared at the long silver necklace lying in Mary's palm.

"It's St. Christopher. It was your mother's."

Laura took the chain and turned the pendant over. The name Delilah was etched into the back.

"It was a gift from her father before he died."

A grandfather she would never know anything about. Tears burned behind Laura's eyes and slipped onto her cheeks. "Thank you."

"What should we do with the doll?" Drew pointed toward the doll on table.

"I'll burn it with the cleansing fire. Whatever power it might have had will be extinguished."

Drew nodded, then led Laura toward the door. Without a backward glance, she picked up her umbrella and walked out of the store.

A deep ache sat in the pit of Laura's stomach. Someone had lied about her mother being here. It was malicious and cruel and whatever was going on here, it wasn't healthy and it wasn't safe. Mary was right. There was nothing left for her here. Not anymore. Her life was in California.

But how had Mary known she'd grown up in San Francisco?

Wariness and suspicion wormed their way into Laura's thoughts, but she pushed them away. This was a small town. In small towns everyone knew everything about everybody. She now had what she came for. She didn't know what had happened to her mother, and she probably never would. But she knew she'd been loved. That she'd mattered. It was time to go home and put all this ugliness behind her.

Chapter 11

Laura watched the rain beating against the street and opened her umbrella.

"So where to next?" Drew asked as he stepped up next to her.

"I'd rather not go back to Lionsheart."

Drew's eyebrows lifted in surprise. "Are you sure?"

Laura nodded. "Mary is right. Without my mother, I don't belong here. It's time I went home and put all this behind me."

A mixture of relief and trepidation shone in his gaze.

She gave him a reassuring smile. "Don't worry. I know it's for the best. You've been trying to tell me that, I just needed to accept it and now that I have, I need to go home. But until then…"

"How about we try the Inn?" He pointed at the white clapboard home across the street that had been restored and turned into a bed-and-breakfast. Rocking chairs beckoned on a wide welcoming wraparound porch. Pots of hanging red begonias blew back and forth with the wind. Laura nodded and they ran side by side across the street and up the front steps as the cold rain battered them.

On the porch, Laura shook off the excess water before stepping inside. The bell rang and Laura cringed as they dripped across the gleaming mahogany floors while walking toward a large counter along the far wall.

"Oh, my, look at the two of you," an older woman with short red hair and very green eyes said as she entered from a back room. "You're soaking wet. Must be pouring cats and dogs out there."

Drew wiped water from his face. "I'd have to agree with you there. We'd like your nicest room."

"Of course. How long will you be staying?" The woman pulled out a large leather-bound book.

Drew turned to Laura, the same question shining in his eyes.

She bit her lip. She knew it was time for this trip to come to an end, to put the search for her mother behind her. She only wished she were ready to put Drew behind her.

"Just tonight. I'll be leaving tomorrow."

She looked up into Drew's eyes and saw approval, and perhaps a touch of regret? She hoped so.

"All right." Smiling, the woman pushed the leather-bound book toward them.

Drew signed his name and gave her a credit card.

"I've put you in the Rose room. It's the room on the right on the third floor. That one has a nice view of the town square." She handed Drew a key.

"Sounds perfect." As he took the key, Laura realized this could be the last few hours they had together.

"Do you have any bags? I'll call Joe to help you bring them up."

"We'll bring them over later," Drew said.

"Oh." The woman looked momentarily confused, then her cheeks pinkened and her smile grew wider.

Heat flushed Laura's face as she realized what the elderly woman must be thinking. And it wasn't too far from what Laura was thinking. If she was going to have to say goodbye to Drew, she'd like to have a nice memory to take with her to keep her warm on those cold San Francisco nights.

"If you'd like to leave your wet clothes outside your door, I'll put them in the dryer for you," the innkeeper continued after Laura finished signing the book.

Laura looked down at her drenched shirt and jeans. "Thank you. I'd appreciate that."

"There will be tea and cookies in the parlor at four o'clock. I hope you enjoy your stay."

"I'm sure we will," Laura said and followed close behind Drew up the stairs to the third floor. As they walked, she took in his wide shoulders and well-defined arms and thought about how strong they'd felt wrapped around her that morning. Saying goodbye to him wouldn't be easy.

Drew unlocked the door and they stepped inside. Their room was large and spotless. The decorations were a bit old-fashioned with an overabundance of pink tea roses, but the bed looked plush and comfortable. She touched it, imagining wrapping herself around Drew and snuggling deep beneath the blankets.

"Take a look at this." Drew stood in the bathroom doorway and gestured her forward.

The deep claw-foot bathtub made Laura sigh audibly. "What I wouldn't give for a hot bath right now."

Drew picked up a book of matches from a tray on the counter and lit a nearby candle. "Why don't you get out of those wet clothes?"

She liked the sound of that.

"Take a nice long bath while I find us some lunch."

Hmm. Laura looked at the flickering candle and

bath oils. Getting out of her wet clothes was exactly what she had in mind.

"You are wonderful. Are you sure?" she asked, though she had no intention of letting him go back out into the storm.

"Absolutely, I'm starving. How's twenty minutes?"

"Great." Laura turned on the faucet and adjusted the temperature.

Drew left the bathroom. "Just hand me your clothes when you're ready."

She was ready now. Obviously he wasn't thinking along the same lines as she was. Was he just hungry? Or was it something else? After their morning together, she'd be surprised if he still wanted to hold her at arm's length. This was their last afternoon together and she wasn't about to spend it alone. She took off all her clothes, gathered them up then walked into the bedroom.

Drew was on the phone talking to his mother, telling her of Laura's change in plans and that they wouldn't be home for dinner. She hoped that meant he planned to spend the next several hours here with her.

"Here you go," she said, once he hung up the phone.

Drew turned toward her, his eyes widening with surprise then quickly darkening with desire as his gaze slid down her body then back up to linger on her breasts. She took a deep breath, lifting them higher. A twitch rippled through his jaw. She couldn't help the slow grin spreading across her face. He did want her.

She handed him the bundle of clothes then slowly walked over to her purse on the bed. With her back to him, she fished inside for a hair clip, piled her hair high on her head and clipped it in place. She glanced over her shoulder. He stood rooted in place, holding her clothes against his chest, oblivious to the spreading wet spot on his shirt while his warm gaze fixated on her.

"Are you sure you wouldn't like to join me in the bath?" she asked with feigned nonchalance.

He swallowed. Then nodded. He opened the door and dropped the clothes in a heap on the floor outside in the hall, then closed and locked the door.

She smiled as she walked back into the bathroom adding what she hoped was an enticing sway to her hips. Hot steam had already filled the room. She poured vanilla bubble bath into the water, breathed in the fragrant scent then stepped into the tub. She moaned with pleasure as the water's heat seeped into her chilled muscles.

Heaven. She sat there for a moment, enjoying the feel of the hot water and the faint smell of vanilla. Drew stood in the doorway watching her. She felt something special with him, something she wanted to explore further, something she didn't want to lose.

* * *

Drew knew this was a mistake the second he stepped into the bathroom. He should go get lunch as he'd planned, but seeing Laura lying there, sudsy bubbles teasing her breasts…looking soft and appealing and incredibly sexy, ate away at his resolve. And killed any appetite he had for food.

He reached behind him and shut the door.

"The water is wonderful." The throaty rasp of her voice heated his body better than any hot bath ever could.

He sat on the rim of the tub. His gaze on hers as he leaned forward and gently touched her lips with his. The softness of her mouth quickened his breath.

She wanted him.

Her desire was a potent aphrodisiac and not one he could resist. She lifted her hand up to his neck, her soft touch leaving a lingering trail of wet bubbles along his skin. The scent of vanilla curled into his brain, mingling with the sight of her bare arm, her skin slick with water.

"You smell delicious," he murmured and tried not to think about her naked body beneath all those suds, but the image of her large breasts, firm belly and rounded thighs, silky smooth and flawless, kept assaulting his mind.

One more kiss then he'd salvage what was left of this situation before he completely lost control. She was on the verge of going back to San Francisco, where she would be safe, and would most likely escape death's touch. He'd be an idiot to give her a reason to stay.

He kissed her again, his mouth moving tentatively over hers as he tried to restrain himself. *Sweet, so sweet.* He ran his tongue over the seam of her lips. She opened to him and he was lost.

With a soft groan, Drew plundered her mouth, exulting in the sensual play of their tongues. A quiver of electric energy shimmered to life and engulfed him with desire. He had to stop. He had to be the strong one.

With a supreme effort of will, he pulled back from their kiss. "I'm sorry," he murmured against the side of her lips, not able to separate himself from her any farther than that. He didn't want to leave. But he had to. Now. Before it was too late.

As if aware of his intentions, she wrapped her arms around his neck, coming half out of the water. Her full breasts were wet and covered in foamy lather that slowly slipped down her skin, revealing the dark cherry red of her nipples. The desire heating his blood exploded within him quickening his pulse, making him sweat.

He slid his hand across her soft, slick breasts, then again over her nipples, loving how they hardened into tight, tempting buds under his palm. Her quick intake of breath did nothing to discourage him. In fact, it recalled to his mind her sweet cries of pleasure when she'd come that morning, and the way she'd wrapped her legs around him so tight, as if she'd never let him go.

He leaned down and circled his tongue around the tip of her left breast, gently pulling the soft peak into his mouth. When he flicked it with the tip of his tongue, she moaned, her nipple growing and hardening even more.

He pulled back as Laura fumbled with the buttons on his shirt. She smiled, her hooded gaze sultry and seductive.

"Are you going to join me?"

She slipped her hand inside his shirt, running her fingers across his chest, lingering on his nipples. Ribbons of heat shot straight through him.

"No," he somehow managed to choke out. "I can't."

"Yes, you can." She leaned forward and unzipped his pants, sliding her warm, wet hands beneath the waistband of his boxers, teasing his skin. He prayed for strength and yet at the same time he wanted her to go lower. To move those hot, slick hands over the length of him.

"The tub," he said in a last-ditch effort at control. "It will be a tight fit." *Merde,* he couldn't seem to catch his breath.

"I'll make room for you," she encouraged and pushed his pants lower on his hips.

An aching heat rolled over him causing his hunger for her to spike beyond reason. Beyond thought.

He captured her face in his hands and plundered her mouth, thrusting inside the warm cavity with his tongue. He stood and let his pants fall to the floor. Her eyes widened as she focused on his obvious desire for her, then darkened with hunger. The pink tip of her tongue slipped out from between her lips, moistening them. He hastily pulled off the rest of his clothes, the need for her pounding through him like a living thing.

She smiled as he stepped into the tub. He pulled her on top of him. Her body, slippery with water, slid across his. A throbbing ache cascaded through him as the softness of her breasts, the firm planes of her stomach and the delicate curls of her womanhood brushed over his erection.

She rose and straddled his hips. He pulled in a sharp breath as she nestled her heat along the length of him. He moved gently, rubbing against her, driving himself a step closer to the edge, and pulling a soft, satisfying moan from Laura.

She leaned forward to kiss him, and he opened his mouth to her and reveled in her passionate touch. She nibbled on the corner of his lips, tasting him, teasing him. She shifted, angling herself over him.

He struggled to grasp one sane thought, a last hold on the real world, the world of pain and loss, the world of reality. The place where he should not be doing this, where caring for someone who was about to leave him and who could very well die was a very bad idea.

And he realized in a jolt of pleasure as she brushed her sweet core over the tip of his penis, that it was already too late. With Laura he couldn't stop himself from jumping headlong into the abyss. There was too much between them, so much more than an attraction or shared childhood memories. And something he would never be allowed to explore because Laura was nearly out of time.

That thought, the one he tried never to allow, shattered his will. He captured her mouth and released his hunger, letting it flow in a storm of passion. His hands skimmed across the lush curves of her body. He wanted to accept her invitation and in one quick thrust end his torment, but he also wanted to make this moment last. He *needed* this moment to last.

He pulled back, shifting so that he pressed against her thigh, and reached for the bar of soap. Sliding it down the groove of her back, he ran the bar over her round bottom and back up again.

He lathered her skin then washed the soap away, exploring her with his mouth. He wanted to know every part of her, taste every inch of her.

She whimpered slightly, a pleasure-filled sound that made his control slip. This would be the last time, he told himself. The last time he held her, touched her. Tomorrow she'd be gone.

The thought filled him with a burning urgency. A need to show her how much she mattered to him.

He had to make the afternoon feel as if it would never end.

His fingertips skimmed her breasts and she arched her back, pushing herself into his hands. He lifted her above him, drew her soft, supple skin into his mouth. She tasted sweet and clean and smelled of vanilla. Yes, he was falling for her, falling hard. And he wanted to touch, to taste all of her.

He sloshed water over the side of the tub as he tried to reach more of her.

"Let's say we move this to the bedroom," he said, as he captured her earlobe between his teeth, and ran his fingers up the inside of her thigh.

She murmured a lust-filled moan that was almost incomprehensible.

Drew eased himself out of the tub and wrapped himself in an extra-large plush towel. Laura watched him, her languid eyes hooded with desire. He pulled another towel out of a basket and held it open for her. She stood and stepped out of the tub and into the soft cotton. He moved it gently across her skin, drying her arms, rubbing the towel down her neck, her breasts, everywhere he wanted to kiss.

And would kiss. And taste.

He bent his knees, dragging the towel down her stomach and pulled her to him, pushing his tongue into her navel, swirling it round and round. He pulled the towel down her thighs, her calves then back up again to the dark silky hair between her legs.

Hungry for the taste of her, he pressed his face against her, thrusting his tongue between her curls to lick her sweet, tender flesh. She grabbed his shoulders, her fingers kneading his muscles as she struggled for balance.

She moaned, her breaths coming in shallow little gasps as she swayed on her feet. She was close, too close to reaching that sweet abyss. He stopped, pulled away and lifted her into his arms then carried her to the bed.

He would not give up control.

Not yet.

Too many emotions and sensations pulsed through Laura as Drew carried her to the bed. Like the perfect way her body fit his, or the way his touch felt against her skin. She burrowed herself within his arms and breathed in his musky scent.

Gently, he bit down on her nipple. She closed her eyes as a sudden shock of pleasure shot through her.

"Do you like that?" he asked in a raspy voice as he laid her on the bed.

"I like you," she said, and tapped his chin with her finger. "And everything you do."

He took her finger into his mouth and sucked on it, the swipe of his tongue on the sensitive tip sending an erotic rush coursing through her. He moved down her torso, leaving a trail of kisses to stoke the fires that were already burning out of control. Once again, he thrust his tongue into her navel, and silently she prayed he'd keep going lower.

Instead, he rose back up next to her, his hands stroking and caressing until she thought she'd scream from frustration. She could play this game. She reached out and traced the ridges of his tight abdomen. He took excellent care of himself, his skin tight and bronzed, his legs strong and sleek.

With a light teasing touch, she moved her hand downward, playing in the soft strands of his hair. She brushed the tip of his penis, watching it jump. Then circled it and took the length of him in her grasp. He felt smooth, yet strong, and she gave him several long, featherlike strokes until he was breathing hard and pulling her up tight against him.

"Drew, tell me you want me to stay." She tightened her grip.

He trailed his slender fingers down her stomach to linger in her silky hair. "You have to go. We both know it."

She shifted, bucking her hips, pushing herself against him.

"You have to go back to San Francisco where you'll be safe."

He leaned down and worked magic with his mouth. Magic more powerful than potions or voodoo dolls.

It didn't take long before she was teetering on the brink. He slipped a finger inside of her, making her rigid with need.

"You don't play fair," she whispered and shifted, rolling her hips.

He probed and stroked, sliding in and out. Sweet tension tightened her chest, squeezing the breath from her lungs. She had to have him inside her. Now.

"Please, Drew!"

He slid into a condom, then rolled her beneath him and, in one quick movement, buried himself within her. She gasped, and pulled her legs up as he filled her. Almost too much for her to handle, but then he started to move and she expanded, the sensation sweetly delicious.

Closing her eyes, she started rocking, their easy movements unhurried like a dance, moving in time to the rhythm of her pulse. She lifted her legs even higher, wrapping them around him, cradling him, pulling him deeper.

How could she go back to San Francisco and give this up? Give him up? He slipped his hands in hers and held on tight.

His pace quickened and fire shot through her, heating her to the boiling point and stealing her breath. She could no longer think or worry, she could only feel the desire building within her, the insatiable need for his sweet, strong touch.

Suddenly, she was climbing, surging on a wave of

passion that was sure to break and send her crashing. With a primal cry, she let loose. He stiffened. He was right there with her. Hand in hand they fell headlong into a deep well of pleasure.

And as Laura lay lost somewhere between sweet bliss and brutal reality, she knew that in life there were some things worth hanging on to, some things worth fighting for and Drew was one of them.

How could she leave him?

Chapter 12

Drew lay back against the pillows as Laura nestled up against him. She felt so good in his arms. He knew as he wound his fingers through her long, silky hair that he'd let things go too far. He cared too much. A lot more than he should.

"Do you think Mary's right?" Laura lightly stroked his chest firing his nerve endings and stirring the embers of his desire once more. "Do you think my mother's dead?"

He avoided looking into her eyes and dropped his gaze to the valley between her breasts. He didn't want to see her pain, didn't want to feel the tenderness she was invoking in him.

He didn't want to fall in love with her.

"I think...something must have happened to her or she would have contacted you."

She took a deep breath, her breasts pushing against him. "I know this sounds crazy, but I'm almost relieved."

This time he did look at her.

"What possible reason could she have had for leaving me alone in another city?" Laura explained. "Whatever excuse she could have given me, it wouldn't have been good enough. I'd always believe that I wasn't loved enough. This way, if she is dead, then she couldn't have come back for me. It hadn't been her choice to abandon me."

Her heartfelt words broke through the wall of distance he was trying to build around his heart. He wrapped both arms around her and squeezed. "Laura, your mother's decisions don't define who you are. She was an adult. It was her life. Good or bad, whether or not she abandoned you, those were her choices to make. They are no reflection on you. Just because she left doesn't mean you weren't good enough or loved enough."

He paused for a long moment. "Sometimes no matter how much you care you can't change what's going to happen."

"I understand that, but if she is alive then her choice left me alone without a family." Her voice stung with betrayal.

"I'm sorry."

"Don't be. It's okay. *I'm* okay." She pushed up onto one elbow and looked down at him. He lifted his head and kissed her, slowly, softly and wished, not for the first time, that they were anywhere but here in this swamp. But they weren't, and because of that, Laura could die.

"I don't know about you, but I'm starving," he said, realizing he needed to distance himself from her both emotionally and physically. "How about I run over to Mabel's and get us some burgers?"

"You're on as long as I don't have to go. Facing that woman once in a lifetime is enough for me."

"What can I get ya?" Mabel asked as Drew approached the counter.

He placed an order for two burgers with the works, including fries and milk shakes. He watched Mabel warily as she rang up his order, and couldn't help wondering how she and everyone else in town could have made the leap that Delilah was responsible for Paul's and Georgette's deaths.

"Mabel, I need to ask you a question about Charlie."

Her gaze hardened. "What about him?"

"Is he dangerous?"

She stared at him for a long moment, her wiry gray hair shooting out in every direction. Then she let loose a loud laugh that started down deep in her ample chest and burst forth. “Charlie? Dangerous? You’ve got to be yanking my chain.”

Drew wasn’t amused. “He’s been hanging around Lionsheart a lot lately.”

“That old fool doesn’t know whether he’s coming or going. After Georgette’s death, he just lost it. Would go out into the swamp for days at a time, searching for his baby, come back stinking to high heaven. I got tired of it. Got tired of him.”

“He thought Georgette was in the swamp?”

“Don’t know why. He stood right there with me when we buried her. Says he sees her walking through the mist. The man’s done lost his mind.”

“You don’t sound too shaken up about it.”

“There’s nothing you can do to help the lost souls or the dead.”

The insane glint in her eyes made Drew’s skin crawl.

“But if you’re worried about that young miss of yours, don’t be. Charlie knows the difference between Delilah and her young’n. Even if they’re so alike. Brought back bad memories for me, though, things I’d rather not think about. Will she be leaving soon?”

He nodded.

“Can’t say I’m not pleased.”

Drew wasn’t surprised. “Why was everyone so sure Delilah had something to do with Paul’s accident?”

“We weren’t. Not until the sheriff pulled the car up out of the swamp and found an *Enemy Be Gone* doll in Paul's pocket. Only one person around here made those. His lovin' wife," she added with a sneer.

"And that was enough to convict her in the eyes of the town?"

"She was planning on leaving Paul. She had a lot of money stashed away in a New Orleans bank account, and she'd bought two one-way tickets on a flight the next day. And guess where she was going?"

He stared at her, knowing what she would tell him.

"San Francisco."

"So why didn't the sheriff arrest her?"

"He would have, but she and her daughter disappeared before he could even talk to her. Mighty convenient if you ask me." Her face filled with disgust and she shook her head. "I called the sheriff, told him that girl of hers was back and that I wanted her questioned. I won't have a restful night's sleep until I see Delilah Larame behind bars."

Drew tensed. "What did the sheriff say?"

"That worthless bum said he'd get around to it."

"I've heard Delilah and Paul were planning on leaving together and starting over somewhere fresh."

Mabel's eyes widened with disbelief. "What about her daughter? Was she just going to leave her here? I said *two* tickets."

The boy in the kitchen finished the order and brought it to her. She handed Drew the bags of food.

He shoved napkins, salt and pepper, straws and ketchup into the bags.

"If it makes you feel any better, Laura hasn't seen her mother since she was a child."

Mabel nodded, her fingers propped under her chin as she gave what he said some thought. "Well now, Drew, I can't say that it does."

He wasn't surprised. "Some people seem to think that Delilah's dead," he said bluntly, watching her closely for a reaction.

Her eyes, already sunk into the folds of too much flesh, narrowed into thin slits. "Oh, that's rich."

"Have you seen her?" he questioned. How could she still be angry enough to want revenge from a woman who has been dead for twenty years?

"Everyone's seen her," Mabel spat.

Shocked, Drew processed her words then quickly gathered his thoughts. "When? Is she still living here?"

"Everyone has caught sight of her in the swamp every now and then. When the moon is full she likes to sacrifice chickens to the demons she worships."

Drew blew out a breath he hadn't realized he'd been holding. "Mabel, Delilah wasn't a voodoo priestess. It was an act, a ruse to help bring business into Voodoo Mystique."

He could tell by the tightening of her mouth that she wasn't buying it.

"I've *seen* her in the swamp," she reiterated. "And I'm not the only one."

Drew paid for the food then left the diner, hurrying down the street, a sourness turning his stomach. Was Delilah alive? Did Mary know? Had she lied to them?

Whether or not Delilah was alive, someone had arranged to bring Laura back just in time for his so-called "awakening" ceremony.

He thought of what Mabel had said about Paul and the *Enemy Be Gone* doll. Had someone really killed Paul? Had they given him the doll as a way of marking him for death?

A chilling thought swept through Drew's mind. Was the person who left that doll in Laura's drawer the same person who put a similar doll in Paul's pocket?

A ceremonial doll used to aid the spirits in finding the chosen one.

The one chosen to die?

Was that their plan for Laura? Was that why he had the vision of her death?

Anxiety twisted inside him, urging him faster.

Was that what his mother had been up to? Was his birthday party, his "awakening" actually a voodoo ceremony? Was she doing all this for him?

Why hadn't Mary mentioned the connection between Laura's doll and Paul's? He had a feeling there was a lot more that she was keeping to herself.

Like why his mother was making an abundance of the same ceremonial candles Mary sold in her store.

He quickened his pace.

Laura had to go back to San Francisco as soon as possible. She would go home, even if he had to take her there himself. He wouldn't be the reason for whatever it was her malevolent stalkers had planned for her.

As Drew took the Inn's porch steps two at a time, he was suddenly sure he'd been gone too long. He shouldn't have left Laura alone. Rushing through the front door and up the three flights of stairs, he burst into their room.

"Laura?" he called, a slight panic in his voice when he saw the empty bed.

"In here," she called from the bathroom.

He inhaled a relieved breath and slowly let it out. She was fine; everything was fine. He crossed the room to the small table in front of the window, removed a vase of fresh flowers and set out their food.

"That sweet lady downstairs dried my clothes just like she promised," Laura said, as she came out of the bathroom. She was dressed and positively glowing.

"That's too bad," he said, and winked as he tried not to let her see his distress. "I was hoping you'd still be wrapped up in a towel."

He picked up his shake and took a long sip, trying

to decide how much, if anything, to tell her about Mabel's tirade.

Laura sat at the table across from him and unwrapped her burger. "I'd like to get back to Lionsheart and pack my things," she said, surprising him. "You and Mary are right. It's time I went home. I called the airlines while you were gone and booked my return flight for ten tomorrow morning."

Relief spread through him as thick and slow as the air moves on a hot August Louisiana afternoon.

"That would be best," he said slowly, though he couldn't help the small ache in his chest. He would miss her.

"Would you mind staying here with me tonight and driving me to the airport?"

"I'd love to." And he would.

"So, I was thinking," she said, and plopped a ketchup-smothered fry into her mouth, "that maybe after your big 'awakening' you could fly out to San Francisco and let me show you around for a few days."

Her tone and actions appeared casual, but he could see apprehension in her eyes. She was worried that, like the others, he wouldn't come back for her.

"I'd like that," he answered.

"By the way, what is this whole 'awakening' thing?" Her big blue eyes held his steady.

"Before today I'd thought it was a birthday party."

"But now you're not so sure?"

"Those candles my mother made by the cartload this morning are ceremonial. I'm not sure what to think."

"She did say something about a man who is turning thirty finding his true nature."

"That's what I was afraid of. And then there's you," he added. "And why you're here."

"You think it could have been your mother who called me, who wanted me here for some kind of ceremony?"

He wiped a hand across his chin. "All I know is that your arriving at the same time as this big 'awakening' can't be a coincidence."

"She could have just sent an invitation. I would have loved to come and meet everyone. Why the deception? Why would she get my hopes up about finding my mother?"

"I don't know. Maybe she wanted to give you a compelling reason to stay."

As Drew downed his burger, he tried to recall all the conversations he'd had with his mother lately, anything that would give him a clue about this party, but he came up with nothing.

It didn't matter. Laura was going home. Soon this would all be over. "You ready to go back to Lionsheart?"

"No," she said, but picked up her shake and stood.

* * *

Drew slowed the car as he rounded the bend in the narrow road, thankful that the rain had finally stopped and the roads were quickly drying. He forced his gaze to the top of the house even as dread squeezed his chest. There was a flicker of movement in the attic window. *Paul?*

Drew narrowed his eyes and stared at the dirty glass set deep beneath the steep roof. This time nothing moved behind the glass, human or otherwise.

He pulled around back and parked the car beneath long tendrils of Spanish moss. The rain has ceased, but the dark clouds left a gray pallor over the late afternoon making the house seem even more ominous.

They got out of the car and skirted the overgrown camellia bushes as they walked toward the back door. The scent of sickly sweet flowers along with an undertone of rot and decay filled Drew's nose. He would be glad when this trip was over.

They walked through the back door and into the kitchen. Two big boxes of candles waited by the door. His mother walked into the room, surprise flickering in her eyes.

"I didn't expect you back so soon."

"Do you need help with these?" he asked.

"Yes, if you could put them in the back of my car, I'd appreciate it."

Laura stepped farther into the room. "Martha, I

just came by to pick up my things, but I wanted to thank you for welcoming me and letting me stay. I really appreciated it."

Martha's forehead crinkled with confusion, then she broke into a wide smile. "Of course, dear. You're like family. You're always welcome here." She pulled Laura into a warm embrace. "I'm so sorry to see you go so soon. Promise me you won't stay gone so long next time."

Those had to be the exact words she'd always longed to hear. Drew only wished he could believe his mother meant them.

"I promise," Laura said, and smiled.

"Are you sure you can't stay for dinner?"

"No, we'll probably eat at the Inn," Drew said. "We want to make it an early night, since we'll be heading out at dawn to catch Laura's flight in the morning."

"Oh." Martha pouted with disappointment. "I was hoping to have you sample some new desserts I've prepared for tonight. Any chance you two can come by later? I won't keep you too late, I promise. It would really mean a lot to me."

Drew picked up a box. "We'll see what we can do."

"Thank you, sweetheart. It was good to see you, Laura. Please be sure to keep in touch."

"I will," Laura said as Drew and his mother walked out the door.

"Where are you going with all these candles?" Drew asked as he placed the box in her trunk.

"Just over to Jeanne's to decorate the hall. I want everything to be perfect for your party. A man doesn't turn thirty every day."

Drew forced a smile. "You're going through too much trouble."

"You're my only son. It's never too much trouble."

"I just drove by Jeanne's and it didn't look like anyone was home."

"It doesn't matter. I have a key." She opened the car door and got behind the wheel. "By the way, I guess it doesn't matter now, but I called the locksmith and he'll be out to change the locks tomorrow afternoon."

"Thanks, *Mère*." He bent down and kissed her cheek.

She looked up at him and cupped the side of his face in the palm of her hand. "It's so good to have you home, Drew. I've missed having you here. I hope after your party you'll realize how much you miss everyone and you'll be compelled to stay."

Drew didn't know if it was her words or the way she looked at him, but a fist of fear clenched his gut.

She smiled then started the car.

"Hold on a second while I go get the other box." He ran back into the house. As he picked up the second box, the scent of vinegar from the candles filled his nose. These weren't ordinary candles and, for reasons he couldn't grasp, he didn't believe for a second she was going to Jeanne's to decorate the hall for his birthday party.

He turned to Laura. "I'm going to follow my mother. Will you be all right here for a little while by yourself?"

Laura nodded, and poured herself a glass of iced tea. "I'll be fine. That will give me time to pack up. Do you want me to pack a bag for you, too?"

"That would be great," he said and gave her a quick kiss before hurrying back out the door.

He'd only be a few minutes, he told himself as he carried the box of candles out to his mother's car. Only long enough to make sure she was actually going to Jeanne's as she'd said. He placed the second box of candles into the trunk and slammed the lid. Then waved as his mother drove down the drive. He watched her car disappear and tried to ignore the foreboding skipping down his spine.

He didn't believe his mother was as fine with Laura's leaving as she pretended to be, nor did he think she was on her way to Jeanne's house.

So what, exactly, was she up to?

Chapter 13

The door banged shut behind Drew as he left the house. The sound echoed through the kitchen, leaving a deafening silence in its wake. Laura stood still, listening, feeling the oppressive weight of the empty house bear down on her. She couldn't stay here alone! She ran to the door to call Drew back, and watched his car disappear from view.

She was too late.

She shut the door then turned back to face the empty room. She was alone in this house. She set her glass of tea in the sink and hurried upstairs to pack. Heart beating too fast, she rushed down the hallways and into her room.

She flung open her closet door and pulled out

her suitcase, trying not to think about the voodoo shrine in the attic or the way she'd been mysteriously locked in the darkened stairwell. Nothing was going to happen to her while Drew was gone. The house couldn't hurt her she assured herself then thought of the phantom burn on her hand after she'd touched her mother's doorknob.

It hadn't been real.

She threw her clothes from the closet into her opened suitcase then turned and faced the dresser. She hesitated, her hand hovering over the top drawer. Her blood raced. Sweat dampened her palms. *There's nothing in the drawer. No snakes or gris-gris, jujus or disfigured dolls.*

Nothing.

She sucked in a breath and pulled open the drawer. Relief swept through her as she stared at her pajamas and underwear.

"See," she said out loud. "Nothing to be afraid of."

Tension seeped out of her as she emptied the drawer. Systematically, she finished packing her things. She picked up the small doll she'd found in the bin in the attic and placed it in her bag. The doll would be a nice accompaniment to the pocket doll she had at home and something she could remember her mother by.

She thought of her mother's photos hanging in the hall and knew the perfect spot for them in her condo back home. She'd have to stop by Jeanne's house on the way back to the Inn and ask Martha if it was okay to take them.

She gave the bath and bedroom one last check then walked down the hall to Drew's room, pulling her bag behind her. As she walked through the door, her gaze immediately went to the rumpled bed. Had it only been last night when, terrified over the snake, she'd asked Drew if he would stay with her? Now she didn't want to sleep without him.

How had he become such a big part of her world so fast?

Was she as important to him? She wished she could be sure. But once she went back to San Francisco, chances were she'd never see him again. The thought brought a deep ache to her heart, but if Drew truly cared for her, if they really did have a chance at a future together, then he'd come for her.

And if he didn't? She pushed away the painful doubts. She didn't need to live with doubts any longer. People could surprise her. She hadn't been abandoned. There was no reason to believe she couldn't be happy. Her mother hadn't left her. She hadn't been able to come back for her.

She was dead.

Laura's throat tightened and tears burned behind her eyes. She had come to this house with high hopes and expectations that she'd find her mother, that they'd get to know one another again and Laura would no longer be alone.

Instead all she'd found was death and misery.

And love?

She sighed. She hoped so.

She walked over to Drew's closet to pack his things and opened the door. An old baseball glove and ball sat on the top shelf. As she stared at the ball, she felt certain it was the same ball that had scared her in the attic stairwell.

Had Drew picked up the ball and brought it back here? She tried to remember, but couldn't. A duffel bag sat on the floor. She picked it up and quickly packed his things then shut the closet door behind her and swung the full bag over her shoulder.

There. Done. The sooner she got out of this house, the better. A loud thump hit the closet door. Laura jumped and turned. A muffled thud reverberated behind the door. Had the ball fallen? A lump of dread lodged in her throat as she waited, half expecting the closet door to creak open.

She turned and quickly left the room, pulling her suitcase behind her as she hurried down the hall. She hated this house. The swamp. Everything about this place and she couldn't wait to get back home.

But there was still one thing she needed to do.

Taking a deep breath to strengthen her resolve, she walked down the hall toward her mother's room. She might not get to see her mother, but this was her last chance to see what she might have left behind.

The room drew closer. There was nothing to be afraid of. It was only a room. Nothing more. Yet, every instinct within her screamed to keep going, to pass it by, to grab her mother's pictures off the wall and say goodbye.

Her mother was dead. Whatever had happened to her, whatever secrets were buried in Laura's head, happened a long time ago. Too long ago now to make a difference.

Go. Get out!

The door to her mother's room loomed before her.

Don't go in there.

The voice in her mind grew stronger and more urgent with each passing step.

No!

She stopped in front of the door.

This was it. Her last chance.

I've kept it just how it was when she left, waiting for her to return. Martha's words whispered through her mind.

Through that door was a window into the past, a chance to see her mother's things, a snapshot into the life they'd both lost.

Fingers trembling, Laura reached for the knob.

Drew stayed far enough behind his mother that he could barely see her car in front of him. He hated to admit it, but he wasn't surprised when she turned left down a barely used road instead of following the bend toward Devil's Walk Bridge and the Larames' house on the other side of it.

He knew his mother was up to something. As much as he wanted to ignore it or forget what he'd seen, people didn't make an abundance of voodoo ceremonial candles unless they were planning a voodoo ceremony.

But why hide it? And why lie about going to Jeanne's? The road narrowed to the point that he had to slow to a crawl. Tree branches scraped along the side of the car. He turned a corner then stopped.

The road ended in a small clearing at the edge of the bayou. He was surprised to see several parked cars and pulled in alongside them. He kept to the trees trying to stay out of sight as he hurried toward an array of wooden structures at the water's edge. What was this place? He searched for his mother, his gaze moving through one enclosure after another.

Something was wrong here.

He felt it in the tightening of his gut. There were people everywhere, some in bright jewel-toned robes, others in everyday clothes just like him, making it easier for him to blend in.

Sweat dampened his shirt and his heart kicked up a beat as he moved among people bustling about tending to goats, sheep and chickens kept in wire cages. Under a thatched roof with a tall center pole, a long bench held statues of saints, dried flowers, candles and incense and looked a lot like the altar he and Laura had found in the attic.

So similar, in fact, that it was clear whose altar this was.

He stepped into the structure and approached the long wooden table. There was a picture of him propped up against a candle. His stomach lurched, turning as if something foul was moving through him.

What looked like a curly lock of his hair was draped over the frame. He stiffened, rubbing his sweaty palms on his pants. He reached out to grab the hair, then pulled back as he noticed the bones, shiny and worn from too much handling lying beneath the picture.

He had to do it. He couldn't let them have a piece of him to use in whatever sick games they were playing. He tried again, reaching out. Hesitating. *It is just hair.* In a swift movement, he knocked the hair off the frame and onto the ground.

He contemplated turning and running, but knew he couldn't leave it there. He kicked at it with his foot, covering it with dirt. Then scooped up the dirt with the hair in it and clenched it tight in his hand. Whatever spell they'd planned to use on him wouldn't work. He hoped. He closed his eyes and cringed. He was buying into their hysteria.

Revolted, he turned from the altar and left the

enclosure. He saw his mother standing near the water and quickly stepped into the shadows behind a thick thatch of trees. He dropped the hair onto the ground and kicked dirt on top of it, burying it as he watched her pull one of the large ceremonial candles from a bag and place it inside the tall iron holder at the swamp's edge.

She then walked about a hundred feet along the shoreline to another holder and placed a candle there, too. Drew watched her walk toward the woods to yet another iron holder. There were four in all at each corner of the clearing.

Was everything he'd ever believed about his mother wrong?

"You're early," a woman in her mid-forties wearing a deep royal blue robe brushed by him with a large pot in her hand. Had he met her before? He watched her long blond braid swing back and forth as she moved. If he had, he didn't remember her.

He followed her, walking past a pig roasting on a spit, spinning over a fire pit filled with red-hot stones.

"Curiosity got the better of me," he confessed, and forced a wide, friendly smile on his face.

"Well, to be honest most of us weren't sure we could make it happen, but your mom is a very determined lady." She dropped the pot on a long wooden table filled with an assortment of food.

"Wow, looks like we're going to have a great feast. I'm getting hungry just looking at it all."

She smiled, her face lighting up with pride.

"Well, try to hold off a while longer, but if you want to grab a little something when I'm not looking, I certainly won't notice." She winked at him and purposefully turned her back.

He rustled the plastic wrap over a plate of cookies, but didn't take one. Couldn't. He knew he wouldn't be able to swallow.

"Wasn't the party supposed to be tomorrow night?" he asked, taking a chance that she wouldn't wonder at his question.

"It was, but your mom wanted the timing to be perfect, and she's always right about these things, you know. But don't you worry," she said, flapping her hand against his arm. "It will be wonderful. Even with moving up the ceremony, everything has been running like clockwork."

She pulled a large Tupperware platter out from under the table and started moving biscuits into a basket.

Why would his mother move up the party? Better question yet, why hadn't she mentioned it to him?

And then it hit him.

Laura was leaving.

He forced his lips to broaden into a smile, though it felt more like a grimace. "Thank you for everything you're doing. I know it's going to be terrific."

"You're very welcome." She turned back to the table.

Drew quickly looked for his mother before stepping out from under the thatched roof. She was in another enclosure at the water's edge, sitting in a high-back chair while a tall black man painted wavy blue lines across her cheeks.

What the hell was going on?

Drew moved behind the nearest tree, his fingers digging into the bark as he watched. He could see the blue paint vividly, and as he watched he thought he could feel the brushstrokes sweeping across his cheeks. He lifted his hand to his face as the memories sucked him back into a time he'd forgotten.

To a night many years ago.

"The lines represent the water." His mother's voice rose with excitement as she painted his face. "The Great Spirit Kafu talks to me through the water, and after tonight he will talk to you, too. Because we're special, Drew. We've been touched."

Candlelight flickered across her face, giving her eyes a wild, almost demonic gleam. She took him to the swamp, where he lay on an altar made of wood in the water, surrounded by candles. For hours it seemed he lay there, half dreaming, half sleeping until he heard raised voices speaking about Laura, and about how they couldn't find her.

Was something wrong with Laura?

Making sure no one saw him, he slipped off his bench, into the water and tried to follow them back to the house. But he was wet and they moved so much faster than he could. Alone, scared and confused, he ran through the darkness until suddenly he was back home.

His heart pounding, he raced up the stairs. Sounds were coming from Miss Delilah's room. He ran in, stopping just inside the door. Miss Delilah was lying on the floor. Blood covered her head and pooled around her on the floor.

A soft cry exploded from his chest.

Auntie Jeanne stepped toward him.

"Go back to the swamp, Drew."

He couldn't make his feet move. "What happened to Miss Delilah? Is she okay?"

Auntie Jeanne bent down and grabbed his shoulders. Her bony fingers digging into his flesh.

He tore his eyes away from Miss Delilah and stared at his aunt. He noticed how wide her eyes were. And how messed up her hair was. Auntie Jeanne never had messed-up hair.

"Drew," she snapped.

"Wh-what happened to Miss Delilah?" He was too scared to move.

She brushed her thumbs across his cheeks. They came away blue. "Laura needs your help. Go back to the swamp and help her. They're taking her to the graveyard."

He heard what she was saying, but he couldn't stop thinking about Miss Delilah and all that blood. He'd never seen that much blood, not even when cousin Paul shot that pesky raccoon last summer.

"Don't let Laura down, Drew. You're a good swimmer. I've already called for help but they might not get there in time. I have to take care of her mama now. Okay? Do you understand?"

He nodded.

"Good boy. Now go!"

She turned him around and gave him a hard shove out the door.

"Go save Laura!"

He ran out of the house and along the edge of the swamp toward the graveyard. This path was his stomping ground, and even in the dark he knew every step. He heard voices up ahead and saw a small boat out in the water with Laura sitting in the back. Then suddenly someone had a knife. They raised it high in the air. Laura screamed. She jumped out of the boat. Someone had her by the arm, trying to pull her back up, and the knife came down.

Laura sank beneath the water, and all that was left was her red sweater grasped in the man's hands.

They were trying to kill her! Why would they do that? Laura could swim, but she was afraid of the swamp and would never go in it at night. Not even when he double-dared her.

He wanted to yell, to scream for help. But there

was no one to help. The people standing on the shore just watched.

Save Laura! His aunt's voice yelled in his mind.

It was dark. He was far away. They wouldn't see him slip into the water. They were too busy watching the boat row back to shore. Drew plunged in and swam as fast as he could while trying not to splash or draw attention to himself.

He heard Laura thrash in the water. Finally, he reached her. She was scared and tired, but unhurt. He grabbed her, holding her head. For a while they were able to tread water, but then she became so heavy he started to sink with her.

He sucked in swamp water and it burned his throat. He started to cry because he knew he was drowning and he would never see his mom again or his dog or Laura.

His awakening wouldn't be complete, and he would never get to hear the Great Spirit Kafu talk to him.

He felt something against his arm. Then Laura was pulled away from him.

"No!" he tried to scream, but instead swallowed another mouthful of water. The last thing he saw was a bright light, so bright it hurt his eyes, and he wondered if the Great Spirit Kafu was coming for him after all.

Back in the small grove of trees, Drew shook his head to clear the overwhelming feeling of fear and sadness. He rubbed his hands over his face. How could he have forgotten all that? The next morning when he'd woken up in a hospital bed, the nurse had told him that he'd saved Laura. But he couldn't remember why or from what.

And he'd never seen her again. Until now.

Cold terror brushed down his back. Now he remembered.

He'd saved her from these people.

From *his mother.*

Nausea cramped his stomach. He bent over, taking deep breaths until the feeling passed. It had been his mother who had tried to kill Laura all those years ago and who planned to kill her now. He'd stake his own life on that.

"Even with moving up the ceremony, everything has been running like clockwork," the woman had said.

Tonight!

Drew rushed out of the grove of trees and looked once more at the enclosure with the high-backed chair, but his mother was no longer in it. He searched the clearing, his gaze moving through all the outbuildings, over all the people and still he couldn't find her.

Had she seen him? Had she gone to the house for Laura?

Panic sliced through him. Not again! He ran back

toward his car, searching the parked cars along the way for his mother's sedan. But it wasn't there.

Where was she?

He jumped into his car and raced back to Lionsheart not caring about the tree limbs scraping the side of the car, or the rain-washed ruts tearing up the suspension.

"Please be okay," he pleaded, suddenly certain that Laura would be gone when he got there.

Chapter 14

Laura didn't know what she expected her mother's room to look like exactly, but she'd thought it would be dark and dank, and feel like a tomb. What she found was a bright, cheerful room with late-afternoon sunlight pouring in through lace curtains.

The only thing tomblike was a large bouquet of dead flowers sitting on the dresser. They were dry and brittle under her light touch. Why would Martha have left these here to rot? In fact, everything seemed to be exactly as her mother must have left it. If it weren't for the fine sheen of dust covering every surface in the room, it would look as though her mother had only left five minutes and not twenty years ago.

Laura ran her fingers across the silver comb and

brush set sitting on the cherrywood dresser. Perfume bottles and a silver tube of lipstick lay on a mirrored tray. She picked up the tube, twisted the bottom and watched the deep red lipstick rise within its silver canister. The rounded top of the waxy substance was dented, as if it had been dropped.

She focused on the tip of the lipstick. Suddenly she could see her mother swiping it across her lips and smiling at her through her reflection in the mirror. Memories pushed at Laura's mind: her mother putting on earrings, bending over and smelling a big bouquet of white flowers.

Aren't they beautiful? Papa Paul sent them.

An icy breath caressed Laura's cheek.

She shivered and brought a hand to her face. Just as it had earlier in Voodoo Mystique, the sensation that she wasn't alone slid through her—a furtive movement out of the corner of her eye, a shadow, a presence. She stood still and let her gaze slide through the room, but saw no one.

"Mom?" she whispered, thinking for a crazy second that maybe her spirit was there with her.

Then she shook her head and let out a shaky laugh.

She looked at the dead flowers and wondered if they were the same ones that Papa Paul had sent. Then she walked toward the dark wooden canopy bed covered with an abundance of thick plush pillows and framed with filmy white silk hanging from wooden railings. An old-fashioned lamp with a silk shade and crystal beading sat atop a bedside table. Alongside it, an antique frame held a picture of Papa Paul, her mother and herself looking like the ideal, happy family. Laura picked up the picture and ran her finger across the dusty glass, trying to touch the family they'd once been. A small ache constricted her heart.

What had happened to them?

Sadness filled her, making her limbs feel weak and tired. How could everything have gone so terribly wrong? She approached a standing jewelry box in the corner and opened the doors. Necklaces and earrings of various colors and sizes filled the drawers. Her hand hovered over a large moonstone pendant. She remembered this piece. It had been her mother's favorite. She'd worn it all the time.

She picked it up and placed it over her head, holding the pendant clutched within the palm of her hand. She couldn't leave all her mother's things behind. She opened the closet doors. Her mother's long flowing dresses still hung inside. A rainbow of colors in cotton, silk and chiffon shimmered on their hangers.

Again she wondered why Martha would leave all these things here after all these years. How could she still have expected her mother to come back? Laura reached out and touched the fabric of an emerald-green dress.

The sweet scent of gardenias filled her nose, and suddenly she could see her mother clearly, she could smell her favorite perfume, could hear her singsong voice echoing through her mind, "*Shh baby, don't say a word.*"

Her vision shifted. The room tilted.

She remembered being pushed down on the floor in the closet.

Her heart pounded. She broke out in a cold sweat. Memories assaulted her.

"It's okay, baby. Mommy's okay. Stay in the closet."

Someone else was in the room. Her mommy was no longer smiling. She looked angry, then scared. Her wide blue eyes met Laura's before she quickly glanced away.

Something was wrong.

Laura did what Mommy wanted. She didn't make a sound. She didn't move, although her heart hammered with fear.

Back in the present, Laura's stomach heaved. She found herself sitting on the closet floor. She covered her face. She didn't want to see anymore.

Couldn't see anymore.

But she couldn't stop the memories from flooding back, couldn't stop her mother's muffled screams from echoing through her mind—the dark shadow of a man entering the room, large and looming, and full of fury.

Like a rag doll, the man grabbed Mommy and threw her to the floor. Panic gripped Laura, tightening her chest, her throat, her jaw. She couldn't swallow. She couldn't breathe.

She put her hand over her mouth to stifle a scream. Hugging her small knees, she gasped a deep breath and held it. The man picked up the big wooden candleholder.

And then she saw him.

Grandpa Randal? What was he doing? Why was he so angry?

Burning pain from lack of oxygen erupted in Laura's chest. She took in quick, shallow, terrified breaths.

He lifted the candleholder high above him.

Laura turned her head, burying her face in her knees.

A sharp pleading cry. A resounding thud. Laura's hands flew to her ears.

Blood splattered, sending droplets of red across the wooden floor and up the wall. Anguish twisted Laura's heart. A sob caught in her throat. Tears blurred her vision. She burrowed deeper into the closet.

But then he was there. Standing in front of her, bending down. She gasped as she saw his angry face and the blood staining his shirt.

Mommy's blood? His eyes looked scary, and full

of hate and anger. She'd never seen her grandpa look like that before.

He reached for her.

"No!" She pushed her back into the wall, trying to move out of his reach.

He grabbed her arm and yanked her out of the closet. She struggled, pulling back. But then she saw Mommy lying on the floor. Laura froze, staring at the blood covering Mommy's face and hair. Panic and fear rushed through her, filling her up and bursting forth. "Mommmeeee!"

She reached for her mother, but Grandpa Randal wouldn't let her go. He picked her up and threw her on the bed.

"No!" she yelled, struggling and fighting against him. "Let me go! Mommy!"

He put a hand over her nose and mouth. She kicked and thrashed, making him grunt and flinch and swear until darkness tunneled her vision.

Then it was over and she remembered no more.

Hot tears splashing on her hands brought her back to the present, but the bloody image of her mother lying on the floor had been burned in her mind. Randal had killed her mother.

She sat at the bottom of the closet, rocking back and forth, tears streaming down her face as the horrible images faded. She sucked in desperate gulps of air. Fighting the waves of nausea crashing over her, she closed her eyes.

No wonder she'd blocked it all.

"I'm sorry, Mom," she whispered and wondered how she could not have known. How could she have spent all these years waiting and searching for her mother when she saw her die? A sob burst forth and choked her. If she had remembered sooner, Randal could have been punished.

A shudder tore through her. She gasped several deep breaths. He still could be.

She heard a noise and looked up, wiping away the tears on her face and saw Martha standing in the doorway. Laura pushed herself to her feet and tried to pull herself together. She heard Drew calling her name. When she looked back at the door, Martha was gone.

Then Drew was standing there, looking at her with a desperate wildness in his eyes. "Are you okay?" he asked, trying to catch his breath.

"She's dead," Laura whispered, feeling slightly shell-shocked. She'd known, she supposed. Mary had told her as much, but to actually see it in her mind, to remember that candleholder coming down on her mother's head, to hear the crack of the wood…

Horror seized hold again and reverberated through her.

"Your mother?" Drew asked, looking slightly confused.

Laura nodded then started to shake. Slow-moving tremors that grew until she didn't think she could stand anymore. Then Drew was holding her, his strong arms surrounding her and pulling her against the sturdy wall of his chest. She clung to him and cried, sobbing for the mother she'd lost, for the hope that had died, for the future that had been ripped away from her.

Randal, her grandpa, the man she had loved and trusted, had with one blow annihilated her life, and then gone back to his own as if nothing had ever happened. But the worst *had* happened—to her mother, to her. And she wasn't about to let him get away with it.

One way or another, that man would pay.

Drew held on to Laura, relief cascading through him just from seeing her standing there, her hair disheveled, her eyes puffy and her cheeks stained.

"I'm sorry," he whispered in her ear.

"It was horrible." She pulled back and looked at him with anger blazing in her eyes. "Why did he do it?"

"He?"

"Randal. He hit my mother with a wooden candleholder. He killed her. Right here. I saw it."

Stunned, Drew stared at her, his gaze shifting to the corner of the room. He remembered Delilah lying there, the blood running down her face and pooling beneath her head. "Randal?"

Laura's eyes widened as she followed his gaze. "You saw?"

Drew stiffened.

"You were here!" It wasn't a question but an accusation.

"Yes."

She took a step back from him. Suspicion gleamed like hard brilliant stones in her watery eyes.

"You knew and you didn't tell me? Why?"

"I didn't remember what had happened until a little while ago." He took her hands in his. "Believe me, I didn't know Randal was involved."

He could see her thinking about what he'd said. "Was it really Randal?"

"I was in the closet. I saw him hit her. I saw her lying there. He pulled me out and threw me on the bed then held his hands over my face until I lost consciousness. I couldn't breathe."

A sick feeling twisted through Drew's stomach. "What happened after that?"

"I don't know. I can't remember any more."

Drew dropped onto the side of the bed. He recalled the vision Paul had shown him in the attic. Hands holding down a squirming Laura while someone anointed her head with oil. Was that what had happened here? He looked up to see Paul standing next to Laura, a look of sadness filling his face.

For the first time, Drew wanted to talk to him, to know the truth. All of it. But more than that, he wanted to help his cousin who, in an instant, had lost his whole world.

Who was responsible for all this? His mother? Jeanne? Randal? He thought he knew, but now…

"I'm having a hard time wrapping my mind around all this," he admitted.

"Why? Because Randal's a senator?"

"No, because he's always been like a father to me." He scrubbed his face with his hands.

She sat next to him, placing a hand on his thigh. He put his on top of hers and marveled how close he felt to her after so short a time, but knew it was because of what they'd been through together. A bond had been formed, and even though neither of them remembered it, their hearts had.

"Was Randal the only one you saw?" he asked.

She nodded. "I think so."

"You're sure you didn't see Jeanne? Or my mother?"

"No. Why?" She stared at him, her big vulnerable eyes searching his. "What aren't you telling me?"

He debated how much he should say. She still wasn't safe. And she wouldn't be, not until he got her away from his mother and back on a plane to San Francisco.

"Why would you ask about Jeanne being here?" she pressed. He wished he could kiss her until her trembling stopped and this nightmare ended.

But he couldn't. The nightmare wouldn't be over until she was back home.

"The night we almost drowned, I came back here looking for you." He paused, not wanting to say why, not wanting to explain about the voodoo ceremony... about how he'd lain in the water with his cheeks painted blue waiting for Kafu to speak to him...to enter him.

Soon you'll be able to hear him, too.

"I saw your mother on the floor. Jeanne was here. She told me to go after you. To save you. She said she had to take care of your mother, then she'd send help for us."

Laura stiffened. "Are you saying Jeanne disposed of my mother's body?"

"Perhaps. I don't know."

"If my mother was already dead, wouldn't Jeanne have gone after me herself?"

It had been his birthday. He remembered. His tenth.

His awakening.

"Drew!" Her voice was shrill, demanding. "What if my mother wasn't dead?"

He stood. "Your mother still hasn't been seen in twenty years."

"Neither have I!"

He stared at her for a long moment. "It's possible, but it doesn't matter. We have to get you away from this swamp and away from Randal. He has the power to make sure you never tell anyone what happened in this room."

Laura stood and grabbed a picture off the nightstand. "Come on," she said and hurried out the door.

"Where are you going?" he called as he caught up with her down the hall.

"To see Jeanne."

He faltered. "Haven't you heard a word I've said?"

She kept going, yelling over her shoulder. "Yes. But I need to hear the truth from her lips. I need to know what happened to my mother that night."

"And if Randal's there?"

"Then we'll let him know we're taking him down together."

Chapter 15

"This is a really bad idea," Drew said as they drove toward the Larames'. The muscles tightened around his mouth and he was clenching the steering wheel so hard his knuckles were turning white.

Laura's stomach was tied up in knots. Now that she finally remembered what had happened to her mother, how could she go back home until she found out the rest? Until she knew whether or not her mother was actually dead?

"Confronting Randal and Jeanne tonight is not smart," Drew continued, his tone deeper and more even than usual.

She knew there was nothing logical about the way she was feeling. She was operating on pure unbridled emotion, but it didn't matter. She had to know. She clasped her hands between her knees and tried to keep her voice steady. "I'd like to hear what Jeanne has to say about that night before I go home."

"And if Randal's there?"

"All the better. This way he'll know he's no longer going to get away with what he did. People remember. People know."

Deep creases framed Drew's eyes as he turned to look at her. She could see how worried he was but she needed answers. She *deserved* to know what happened to her mother.

Her stomach turned again. She cracked the window, and closed her eyes as the fresh air hit her face. She had to hold herself together long enough to discover the truth.

The sun sank lower in the sky as Drew pulled up the long driveway. Soon it would be night. How she'd love to get away from this dreadful swamp before then.

She lifted the moonstone pendant still hanging around her neck and a fresh wave of sadness seeped through her. No matter how hard the truth was going to be for her to hear, she wanted to put all this behind her, to move on with her life.

And she wanted to move on with Drew.

She turned to look at him once more. His face was drawn, his lips thin. Finding out what had happened to her family was critical to her, but she knew discovering the truth might cost Drew what little family he had.

Most likely Randal had killed her mom. And if she was having a hard time believing, how hard was it for Drew?

Drew parked the car. As they got out, he pointed toward a flagstone path that led around back. "Jeanne always liked us to enter through the kitchen."

Laura didn't remember that or anything about the house. She felt lost as she rushed to keep up with him. He walked with a rigidity that made her feel as if he towered over her. He was really upset. Perhaps he was right. Perhaps this was a bad idea. If her memories were right and Randal had killed her mother, then surely Jeanne knew about it. How far would a powerful politician and his wife go to keep his secret?

Laura grabbed Drew's hand, hesitating as they entered a brick courtyard next to a large round Cupid fountain. "Do you really believe the Larames are dangerous people?"

Drew stopped and turned to her. "No." There was a long pause. "Maybe. The truth is, I don't know. Everything I thought I knew about everyone has suddenly been turned on its head."

She led him to a nearby bench where they sat close, their thighs touching, their hands clasped. His warm skin against hers made her think about how important he was to her. He had been there for her through this whole ordeal. She wanted to be there for him, too.

"I don't want to push this, Drew. If you don't want to confront the Larames right now, we can wait. We can take what we know to the sheriff and let him deal with it."

Drew stiffened, but nodded. She knew what he was thinking. She knew Randal would rather have Drew confront him than to have to deal with the sheriff. When Drew didn't answer, she took a deep breath and looked around. Why couldn't she remember this place? She was sure that once she'd remembered what had happened to her mother, all her memories would come back. But they hadn't.

She couldn't remember anything that had happened after Randal had held his disgusting meaty hand across her nose and mouth. Shivers of revulsion swept through her. What had he done to her? Why hadn't he killed her, too?

"Are you ready?"

She nodded. They stood and walked toward the back door. Drew knocked and Laura held her breath. She thought again of what she'd seen and heard. She was worried about Drew and what he was going to have to face, but the truth was, she wanted Randal to be here. She wanted him to open that door, because right now she'd like nothing better than to jump down his throat.

A woman dressed in white from head to toe

answered the door. Laura flexed her shoulders, forcing herself to relax.

"We're here to see Randal and my aunt Jeanne," Drew announced.

The woman, some kind of housekeeper or cook, Laura guessed, nodded and opened the door wider.

"The missus is in the garden room." She stepped back as they entered.

"I know the way." Drew walked through the large kitchen and down a hallway where raised voices echoed off the walls.

"We have to do something, Jeanne," a female voice said. "It's all going down right now. We have to get her out of here."

The hair tingled on the back of Laura's neck at the threatening tone.

"Don't you think I know that? Right now, I don't even know where they are."

Laura's breath caught as she easily recognized Jeanne's soft Southern drawl.

Abruptly, Drew turned toward an opened door and came to a sudden halt in front of her. Laura plowed into him, bouncing off his hard back. He stiffened and shifted slightly, blocking the doorway.

The talking in the room suddenly stopped.

"Drew?" Laura heard Jeanne say.

Unable to wait a moment longer, Laura stepped around him.

Jeanne's eyes widened and her mouth dropped

open. Laura's gaze moved to the woman with her. She was nondescript with short silver hair and wore men's clothing.

Instantly, Drew wrapped an arm around Laura's waist, pulling her close to him.

Confused, she looked up at him, but his gaze was locked on the other woman. Laura turned back to her. The woman hadn't moved. She had that frozen, deer-in-the-headlights look about her. As Laura's eyes met hers, the color drained from her face. Her blue eyes filled with fear and a trembling hand flew to her mouth.

"What is it?" Laura asked, not understanding. Her heart kicked into an uncomfortably painful beat.

The woman took a small step forward, her face crumbling. "Laura," she murmured.

Laura wasn't sure if it was the sound of the woman's voice or the pain shining through her very blue eyes, but suddenly her mind grasped the knowledge that her heart had already known.

Her mother.

Tears filled Laura's eyes. After all these years, after all her prayers and sleepless nights crying for her mother, here she stood before her. Her arms outstretched, love and heartbreak beaming from her eyes—eyes that looked so much like Laura's own.

Her head spun. She swayed, her legs weakened. She needed to sit down. Drew tightened his grip and led her to a chair.

"She's too pale. She needs water." Jeanne rushed from the room.

Her mother hurried forward, bent down in front of her and peered into her face. Suddenly, Laura felt vulnerable, on display, like some new species of insect thrust under a microscope. She wanted to turn away, to run, to scream and cry, but she didn't do any of those things. She just sat there and let this woman stare at her. This woman she'd been looking for and wondering about all her life, so certain she must be dead.

Jeanne returned a second later with a glass of ice water in her hand. Laura took advantage of the distraction and turned her attention to Jeanne and the water.

"Thanks," she said, and took a long drink she could barely swallow.

"Are you all right?" Jeanne asked.

Laura stared at her. Was she all right? She'd just found out her mother, who'd abandoned her too many years ago to count, wasn't dead after all but instead stood right in front of her.

She squeezed the glass so tight, she was afraid it would shatter. The anger burgeoning within her must have shown in her expression for her mother stood and stepped back. Her expression was filled with grief. Her entire body sagged. Shoulders slumped, she walked back across the room to stare out the wall of windows as the last of the sun's light faded to night.

"Laura?" Jeanne said again.

"How can I possibly be all right?" Laura asked, her voice sounding shrill. "I had just managed to convince myself that my mother was dead. That she had to be dead, because there was no other possible explanation for her not to have come for me, to have left me alone all these years."

Her mother's back stiffened, but she said nothing as she continued staring out into the night.

Coward. The word rang sharply through Laura's mind.

"So, you've been right here all this time?" she demanded when her mother still didn't turn to face her.

"Yes and no." Finally she turned away from the windows. Tears stained her cheeks and her voice was hoarse with emotion. "I've been living in a town about thirty miles from here, where no one knew me or remembered the name Delilah Larame."

Laura stared at her, her heart clutched tight with pain. "And what about me?" she asked, her voice breaking as she forced out the words.

Her mother stepped forward, one hand outstretched in a pleading gesture. "I wanted to take you with me, Laura. More than you can ever know. But I couldn't take the chance that *she* would find you."

"She? That who would find me?"

"My mother," Drew said.

Laura's gaze shot to him. "What are you talking about?"

When he didn't answer, she looked to Jeanne and then back to her mother. What were they all talking about? "What does Martha have to do with any of this? It wasn't Martha I remember hitting you, it was Randal. Are you telling me I remembered wrong?"

Her mother's head shook slowly back and forth while her gaze swept the floor.

"I thought…I thought you were dead," Laura whispered, still not able to comprehend the sight of her mother standing there in front of her. *Alive and well.*

Jeanne's face twisting with guilt enraged Laura even more. She turned on her. "All these years and you knew the truth. You knew where I was, yet neither of you came for me."

"I'm sorry, Laura." Her mother stepped toward her again, but stopped before reaching her. She clasped her hands, wringing them violently in front of her. "You're right. It was Randal. He did hit me. But it wasn't me he wanted. It was you."

"Me? Why?"

"He was so angry about Paul's death," Jeanne said. "He wanted revenge. He wanted justice."

"He blamed me," her mother added.

"You? Because of that voodoo stuff?"

"Randal didn't know about our plans to leave,"

her mother explained. "Paul was afraid to tell him. It was a mistake. I knew it then, but there was no talking to him. After Paul's death, Randal was so upset he fell for Martha's lies. He wanted someone to blame, needed someone to focus his rage on. I was his choice. After that it was easy for Martha to draw him into her plans."

Jeanne stepped close and placed a comforting hand on Delilah's arm. "When Martha promised him that the voodoo ceremony would guarantee him the governorship...well, I'm ashamed to say he took her up on it."

Drew cursed under his breath. He clenched and unclenched his hands, and that telltale muscle in his jaw was twitching a jig. He was livid.

"Don't look at me like that, Drew," Jeanne commanded. "Randal was a man full of grief and rage."

"You can make excuses for him all you want, but he participated in trying to kill a little girl." Drew spat the words. "How could you forgive him for that?"

Jeanne's eyes filled with tears. "Because I had lost my only son. I was all alone and I couldn't lose him, too. He was the only family I had left. He didn't mean to do it. He was consumed with evil and rage. He still has nightmares over what he did."

"And the fact that he did indeed win the governorship and from there went on to become a U.S. Senator was only icing on the cake." Drew's voice grated.

"What about my nightmares? Who did I have to help me?" Laura demanded.

"I did everything I could to save you and your mother," Jeanne insisted. "I called the authorities. I sent Drew after you and, as soon as I could, I whisked you out of the hospital and sent you to San Francisco to the same boarding school I went to as a child. I am an alumni there and a member of the board. I made sure you never wanted for anything. But most of all, I made sure Martha could never get to you."

"You're right," Laura said through clenched teeth. "I never wanted for anything. Except for a family. There was no one to visit on the holidays. No home to go to. After the first year, the dean took pity on me and took me home with her!"

Jeanne's hand flew to her hips. "We did the best we could, Laura. Your mom had to be hospitalized, too. I drove all night taking her to Arkansas so no one could find her. Then I had to drive all the way back here to get you to San Francisco and safety. I'm sorry if it wasn't your idea of utopia, but you're alive today because of it."

"How dare you—" Seething, Laura could no longer speak. Her heartbeat raced, and an uncomfortable heat surged through her.

"Laura, I love you," her mother said, stepping toward her once more. "I always have. I just wanted you to be safe. Jeanne and I both did."

Laura inhaled a deep breath and tried to calm

her nerves. "You were scared. It was a bad scene. I understand that. In a rage, Randal tried to kill us, but we both survived. No one found you, so why not come for me? After a week? A month? Even a year? Why didn't anyone ever come for me?"

Tears of torment and rage stung Laura's eyes. She blinked them back, refusing to let these women see how badly they had hurt her.

"Please, Laura, believe me," her mother pleaded. "I would have come after you if I could have. But I had to live in hiding, in a shack in the swamp. I didn't want you to have to live that way, never being able to go to school, never being able to make friends. You were so much better off in the city with Jeanne taking care of you."

"How do you know how much better off I was? How do you know anything about me? You weren't there." The air whooshed from Laura's chest. She couldn't take any more. She had to get out of there. She turned toward the door.

"Wait!" Jeanne commanded. "Laura, you can't go."

"Oh, now someone wants me to stay!" She whirled back on them. "Tell me, why should I? You haven't said anything that has made any sense." She turned to her mother. "You could have left this place," she accused her. "We could have gone anywhere."

"I couldn't let her find us. She *knows* things. I had to stay and watch her."

Disbelief filled Laura as she stared at her. "No, you didn't. What you had to do was take care of me. I was *your* responsibility. *Your* child."

Her mother crossed the room until she was standing only a few inches in front of her. She reached out and touched the moonstone pendant hanging from Laura's neck. Laura stiffened, but didn't move.

"Why do you think you're here now?" her mother said softly. "She has never let you go. You are the key to her plans for getting what she wants. She won't stop until you're dead."

A chill seeped down to her core. "That's ridiculous. I don't even know *who* you're talking about."

"My mother was the one who called you, Laura," Drew stated from the corner of the room. "She was the one who brought you here."

"Why?" And why was he just telling her this now? She stared at him, a worm of wariness moving through her. What else had he been keeping from her?

"Martha needed you here to complete the ceremony," Jeanne added.

"Does she know you're still alive?" Drew asked Delilah.

"I'm sure she suspected. I disappeared. And like I said, she *knows* things."

Knows things. Laura could have laughed out loud if she wasn't so furious. She fixed her eyes on the door. She wanted out—out of this house, this state, this madness. The mother she'd been wishing for all these years was a crazy woman.

"The ceremony has been moved up to tonight," Drew said. "They know Laura is leaving in the morning."

"Tell me you're not buying into all this?" Laura demanded.

"This is the truth you've been searching for, Laura. It wasn't Randal that wanted you dead that night. It was my mother. We need to get you out of here tonight."

Laura stared at him. This couldn't be true. "Are you saying it was your mother all along? She's the one who tried to run me down? And the note? The snake? I don't understand. Why would she want to hurt me?"

Drew's gaze hardened before it shifted away.

Suddenly he looked guilty.

How stupid was she? Was *he* in on it all along?

"No, I'm afraid that was me," her mother said, and at least had the good grace to look ashamed. She dropped into the nearest chair. "I'm sorry. I wanted you to go home. I was trying to scare you into leaving. You don't scare easily."

"No, she doesn't," Drew said. "How was Charlie Wallis involved in all this?"

Laura's head was spinning. She stared back and forth between them, trying to understand how she'd gotten so far off track. All she'd come here for was to find out if her mother was dead or alive, and somehow she'd gotten sucked up into some weird conspiracy. Her mother, who she'd hoped was alive, had been doing everything she could to scare her into going home.

Laura's stomach turned.

"Charlie and I live together," her mother explained. "He's been trying for years to find proof that Martha was behind his daughter's death. He's cultivated and maintained the image of an old derelict, hoping people would let their guard down around him and speak freely without thought to his presence."

"Has it worked?"

"Well enough to discover their plan to bring Laura back."

Laura cringed, realizing how easily she'd been manipulated. "And Mary? Was she in on it, too?"

"Yes."

Laura shook her head. "I should have known. You can tell her for me that she's a very convincing liar."

"It wasn't like that," her mother insisted. "No one wanted to deceive you. We just wanted you to be safe."

Laura's hard gaze met hers. "The only person who has tried to hurt me, Mom, is you."

Chapter 16

His awakening.

It was all becoming clear to Drew now. The ceremony tonight was a re-creation of the night when Laura almost died. This was all about him being awakened to some voodoo spirit. *The Great Spirit Kafu talks to me through the water, and after tonight he will talk to you, too.*

Paul stood in the corner, glaring at him with frustration. All these years, Drew had blocked him and the other bothersome spirits, but perhaps they had been trying to tell him something he needed to know.

Something that could have stopped what was happening now.

He hadn't listened. He'd turned his back on them and now it was too late. Try as he might, he could not hear them.

"It's not me who wants to hurt you, Laura," Delilah insisted. "It's Martha."

Laura's lips thinned as she pressed them together. "Fine. What does Miss Martha want from me?" she asked through a clenched jaw.

"Your blood," Delilah said softly.

Drew cringed. Why couldn't Delilah leave well enough alone? Nothing was going well, tonight. And nothing would until Laura went back home. She should do now what she should have done then, put her daughter in the car and drive away.

Far away.

"This is ridiculous. You all are ridiculous," Laura said.

"My mother is a voodoo priestess," Drew explained, and plowed a hand through his hair. Maybe if he could just get it all out, get this conversation over with then she'd go. "The real deal. That's why you need to get out of here. Right now."

"Oh, please," Laura said. "Do you take me for a complete fool?"

"When I followed her earlier, I saw her getting her face painted blue, and then I remembered what had happened the last time I saw her like that."

"Yes, I saw her, too, with funny blue lines on her face. But that hardly means—"

"You mean you saw her when you were young?" Jeanne asked, alarm ringing in her voice.

"No, tonight. In the doorway of my mother's room."

"What?" Drew said, suddenly as alarmed as Jeanne had sounded. "Did she say anything to you?" Why hadn't his mother grabbed her right then and there?

"No. One minute she was there, and the next I heard you calling for me."

"She must have hid when she heard me. She was probably coming for you."

Laura stared at him, her eyes hard. She didn't want to hear any more, he could tell. She was shutting down, pushing it all away.

"She needs you to complete the ritual," he said, trying to make her understand.

"What ritual? For what?"

"For Drew's awakening," Jeanne answered.

Drew clenched his fists. He was the reason for everything that had been happening, and yet he'd been unable to stop to it. He'd known about the awakening. His mother had told him, but he hadn't listened. He hadn't cared.

He hadn't tried to understand.

"Twenty years ago, Martha started a ritual, inviting the spirit of darkness, Kafu, into Drew's body," Jeanne explained, and tapped two fingers against her chest. "His essence lives there now, Drew. A fine thread that connects you to him and has since that night. He needs the sacrifice of a child, not just any child, but one with a mystical lineage. Then he becomes you. And you become him."

"Your power will be absolute," Delilah said softly, her eyes haunted. "Unfortunately, Laura has that lineage through her father."

"I never even knew my father," Laura whispered.

"I think I'd know if I had some evil spirit's essence living inside me," Drew said through a rigid jaw.

"He's dormant. Blocked. You wouldn't know of his presence until after the ritual has been completed," Jeanne explained.

"Paul found out from Charlie's daughter, Georgette, who had been a part of Martha's clan, about how the ritual would work the first time," Delilah said.

"They drove to Lionsheart to warn us. Afterward, they were rushing to tell the sheriff when Paul's car went off Devil's Walk Bridge. To this day we don't know if it was a horrible accident or if somehow Martha had killed them. But Paul and Georgette died trying to protect you both," Jeanne said, a look of deep sadness etched onto her face.

"Laura, that night I was planning to take you and disappear," Delilah continued. "We were on our way out of the house when Randal caught us. I'm so sorry, baby. Sorry I couldn't protect you."

Silent angry tears trickled down Laura's cheeks.

"Drew, it's because you can see," Delilah said. "Like your mother, it's your gift and the reason Kafu has chosen you. And why he chose your mother before you."

Suddenly Paul was standing in front of him, yelling in his face, silent, soundless screams with nothing to betray them but the gentle lift of Drew's hair.

Drew turned away from him toward the windows, staring out into the night, into nothing. All of this death and pain because he was cursed.

"Drew, do you see something?" Delilah asked, watching him intently.

"It's Paul," he whispered, finally admitting to them what he'd never wanted anyone to know.

He heard a small cry and peered at Jeanne through the reflection in the glass. She was staring at him wide-eyed, a fist pushed against her mouth.

He turned around. "*Merde,* Jeanne. I'm sorry. I didn't think."

"Why is he here?" she asked, her voice high-pitched and squeaky.

"He's always been here."

"What is he saying?" Delilah's skin had turned the color of ash.

"I don't know," he admitted. "I can't hear him."

"What are you talking about?" Laura asked, clearly confused.

"Drew has visions," Jeanne said. "He has the gift to see those touched by death."

"And those who have died," Delilah added. "Like Paul."

His biggest fear realized, he watched as revulsion twisted Laura's face.

Anger soured Drew's stomach. He didn't ask for this. Didn't want it. Any of it.

Laura shook her head and backed away from him.

"You're saying Papa Paul's been with us, with me, this whole time?" She brought her fingers to her cheek.

"And all those times you told me I was in danger. You told me I was going to die. Was this how you knew? Did you see it? Did you see me die?" Her voice trembled.

He stepped toward her, wanting to tell her that it was okay. But it wasn't and she knew it.

"I didn't know how to tell you."

She moved toward the door, her eyes wide with disbelief, her mouth twisted with anger. "You are all part of some sick delusion. You've obviously lived in the swamp too long. I don't know what's wrong with any of you, but I want you to stay away from me. Do you understand me?"

Drew stepped toward her. "Laura."

"Especially you. Stay away from me."

With tears blurring her vision, Laura ran out into the night. All these years she'd longed for her mother, longed to know what happened to make her mother abandon her. And now that she knew, she wished she didn't.

What kind of mother gave up her only child to "watch" a lunatic? And what about Drew? For all she knew he was in on this whole scheme. His story of seeing dead people and predicting death was crazy.

Perhaps he was the one who lured her back here. So the sacrifice could be complete and he could become all-powerful.

What a bunch of hooey.

All of it. She was surrounded by woo-woo people who were disillusioned and a bunch of liars. Crazy, demented liars who had put a snake in her bed and tried to run her down in the street. What else would her mother have done to scare her into leaving? How far would she have gone? Deep pain sliced through Laura's heart.

And her mother had said she loved her.

Toxic, deadly love that could get her killed.

Her head was spinning. She stopped beside the Cupid fountain and stared up at the sky. Black clouds rolled in, boiling across the first stars daring to show themselves. Another storm was coming. And from the look of things, it would be a doozy.

All the more reason for her to get out of there.

She continued walking down the path. Could Martha really be trying to kill her? Ridiculous. If that was true, Martha had had ample opportunity and hadn't taken it. Something else was going on here, something Laura no longer cared to find out about.

She tried to still her racing thoughts and control the emotions ping-ponging through her, but couldn't. She needed an escape plan. She sat on a bench and dropped her head in her hands.

Good God. Her mother was alive. After all these years. Her mother was alive.

And she'd thrown Laura away as if she were… *disposable.*

Fresh tears filled her eyes and slipped down her cheeks. She should have stayed in San Francisco and never have come back to this godforsaken place.

A large spider scurried up onto the bench next to her. She jumped to her feet. A shudder rocked through her. All this time, and her mother had chosen to live in some shack in this disgusting smelly place rather than live anywhere with her.

All so she could *watch* Martha.

A cold hand brushed Laura's cheek. She stiffened. How many times had she felt that sensation since she'd been here?

Drew can see the dead.

Papa Paul?

Her eyes darted to the shadows in the garden. Was it true? Were there spirits all around her? Suddenly, she could no longer tell what was real and what wasn't. She shook her head and shivered as she walked down winding flagstone paths illuminated by copper garden lights.

None of this is true, she thought. But it didn't matter. *They* believed it was real. *They* believed that spirits and voodoo priestesses were out to get her. It was crazy. All of it. Her mother was insane. *She* was the one Laura needed to get away from.

Jeanne and Mary both bought into her mother's delusions, feeding them. And Randal? She could still feel the terror racing through her as his hand fell over her face. He hadn't killed her mother after all.

It wasn't me he wanted. It was you.

Laura shivered and thought of Drew. Her heart broke as she pictured his face. She had let herself get too close to him, and now she'd pay the price. He was misguided or at the very least delusional. And he'd been the one she'd thought she could count on.

But she was wrong. There was no one here for her. No one left she could trust. All these years hoping, waiting...*wasted.*

She'd let the mystery surrounding her mother infect her entire life. She'd grown up feeling tainted, abandoned, unloved. No wonder she had never been able to find love, to *let* herself be loved. She'd shut down anytime anyone got too close. And then she'd blamed them for leaving.

Boy, was she messed up. And it was her own damn fault for buying into the lie of motherly love—that all mothers love their children unselfishly, unconditionally. It was time she stood on her own and took back the power she'd given her mother over her life.

Laura made her way to the front of the house and to Drew's car, moving quicker as the wind picked up and rustled the trees. She needed to get back to the hotel and then to San Francisco so she could put this mess behind her. She opened the driver's door and climbed inside, hoping Drew had left the keys in the ignition.

No such luck.

She should go back in the house and demand them. But she didn't want to see him again. Not now. Not ever. She needed a cab. Worse, she needed a phone. She stared back at the house. The front door lay in darkness. If it was open, she could slip in, use a phone then slip out again without anyone noticing.

Another gust of wind beat at the car. If she was going to do this, she needed to do it now before the storm hit. She rushed toward the front door, thankful that the porch light wasn't on, and pressed down on the latch. The door opened. Letting loose a sigh of relief, she slipped in and eased the door closed behind her.

Through the first door on the right, she saw the corner of a desk from the dim light of the moon shining through French doors. An office.

She crept inside and shut the door quietly. She clicked on a Tiffany lamp sitting on the corner of the desk. A jumbled pattern of red, yellow and green light reflected eerily across the desk's surface, but didn't reach into the far corners of the room.

Taking a deep breath, she gazed into the darkness, trying to penetrate it. An eight-by-ten picture of Randal and Paul sat on the desk. She stared at their faces, and, once again, wondered how things could have gone so terribly wrong.

A deep ache settled inside her as she thought of the picture of her, Paul and her mother. Her "perfect" family had been an illusion that had never existed. What was real were the people who lived in this house. The man who'd hurt her twenty years ago. And the people in the garden room who'd tried to hurt her now. A shiver cascaded down her back as she realized she was standing in the den of the lion. She was in Randal's office. What would he do if he caught her there now?

She reached for the phone, her fingers trembling above the receiver. She closed her eyes and took a breath to steady her nerves, then dialed Information for the number of the cab company that had brought her out here.

She wrote down the number on a pad nearby and started to dial. Like loud fists banging against glass, a powerful gust of wind beat against the house. The French doors blew open. Leaves, dirt and decaying bits of the swamp swirled into the room and smacked her face. Laura dropped the phone and ran to wrestle the doors shut.

As she stood there, staring out into the night, a sudden certainty settled over her that the swamp and the evil that lay beneath it had no intention of letting her go. That somewhere between the dark and light she'd be trapped, lost in the shadows of the bayou.

A floorboard creaked. Laura whirled around, her limited vision once more searching the dark corners of the room. Icy fingers of fear grasped hold of her racing heart and squeezed. She had to get out of there. Rushing back to the desk, she picked up the phone again and dialed, hoping that the cab company would answer on the first ring. Finally, the line connected.

"I need a cab," she said into the receiver. "Pick me up at the bottom of the drive at Larame Manor." Laura paused as she heard footsteps approaching in the hall. "And hurry. Please. Please hurry."

The French doors flew open once more, blowing damp, foul-smelling debris deep into the room. It felt as if tendrils of the swamp swirled around her, pulling her toward the doors, toward the darkness. Laura stifled a scream, holding it deep within her as once more she pushed the doors shut and this time raised the bolts to secure them into the frame.

Before she could turn around, the light from the Tiffany lamp went out, plunging her into total darkness. Had someone come into the room? No, she told herself. The electricity had gone out. She didn't move. She stood still, straining to listen over the clamor of the blowing wind outside. She had to get out of there.

She took a step forward. The air around her suddenly grew cold. She stopped, frozen in her tracks. Something in the room shifted as if someone had moved. In the corner, shadows darkened and merged.

Fear squeezed her chest painfully. "Is somebody there?" she whispered.

No answer except the deafening drum of her heartbeat.

She moved toward the door, following the cold, hard edge of the heavy wooden desk. A sound stopped her. The hair on her nape prickled. There was someone *or something* in the room with her. She could feel it. A presence.

She strained to hear more over the storm. Breathing. A footstep. Anything.

Randal?

She bolted from the room, from the house and out into the storm. She didn't stop running until she got to Drew's car. The wind ripped at her hair, clawing and pulling like a wild thing. She grabbed her bag from the trunk and raced down the driveway fighting the teetering suitcase, pulling it behind her as it yanked on her arm. The sooner she got away from this place the better.

Because if she didn't get away, she'd die.

And she didn't need Drew's so-called visions to tell her that.

Chapter 17

Possessed.

Was it true?

Somehow Drew'd always known things, had an instinct about which moves to make. It was why he'd always been so successful. Not because of his determination, his hard work as he'd always believed, but because of Kafu.

The thought turned his stomach, sickening him.

Paul was jumping up and down, his mouth opened in a silent scream. He had to get Kafu out of him. But how? And who could he trust to help him? Certainly not his mother.

"We should go get Laura and bring her back."

"She needs a couple minutes on her own," Delilah said.

"She'll have all the time she needs once she's back in San Francisco." Drew walked toward the door. Even though he didn't want to face Laura again, he didn't have much choice. He wouldn't leave her out there alone.

"Why can't you hear Paul?" Jeanne asked, falling into step beside him.

"I learned to block them out a long time ago." He quickened his pace, as Delilah caught up to them. "I'm taking Laura back to the Inn. She has an early flight. If you want to talk to her, to try and explain anything else, you'll need to come by tonight."

By the time Drew entered the gardens, he saw no sign of her anywhere. "Laura!"

No answer.

Paul was furious. Drew could barely make him out at the edge of the garden flickering and yelling, his face a distortion of fury.

"You need to let them back in, Drew," Delilah said as she watched him with eyes that saw too much.

Wind whipped at his hair and thunderous clouds raced across the sky. "No. I don't," he said, raising his voice against the din.

"Paul can help us find her," she insisted.

Can he? "You don't know that."

He *wouldn't* do it. If he let Paul back in, he let them all in. Including Kafu? He took off through the gardens, going deeper behind the house. What if something happened to Laura before he could find her? He should have followed his instincts and taken her directly back to the Inn.

His instincts or Kafu's?

They spent the next ten minutes combing the entire lighted yard up to the tree line.

"Laura wouldn't go into the woods in the dark alone especially with a storm coming in." Drew's frustration grew. They were wasting time. She wasn't here.

"It's time to call the sheriff," Jeanne said. "I'll pull whatever strings I can to get him out here."

"And Mary. Call Mary," Delilah insisted.

As they hurried back toward the house, a knot formed in the pit of Drew's stomach. Laura was gone. This time he'd been too late.

An animal's high-pitched screams filled the air. An owl hooted. A bat flapped overhead, too close. Laura ducked. She looked at the house one more time as the wind tousled her hair. She wanted to go back up the drive and inside to wait, but she couldn't. She'd rather take her chances with the elements than the evil she felt inside that house.

She continued down the drive, refusing to let the darkness enfolding her frighten her as she moved away from the lights of the house. A large splash in the water edging the drive startled her. An alligator? Or some other predator in this death-filled swamp.

A violent shiver shook her.

The animal's squeals ended, abruptly. Laura shivered. The poor thing. There was so much death here. She imagined Lionsheart lurking on the far side of the bayou through the dense foliage and cringed. Her life was unraveling and coming apart at the seams. She didn't know what to believe or who to trust. All she wanted was to go home. And she wanted to go right now.

Mist swirled, blowing across the surface of the water. Frogs and insects whined in a wild cacophony almost as if they sensed the violence of the oncoming storm and were crying out a warning. Their raucous clamor drowned out all other sounds.

It occurred to her that she'd never hear if someone was approaching with all the racket. She'd have no warning. She shot a furtive glance around her, but saw no one.

Not even Drew.

A dull ache pierced her heart.

"Where's that cab?" she said out loud, hoping the sound of her voice would add a sense of normalcy to an impossibly abnormal situation. Instead, the quaver in her tone only increased her tension.

Nothing in her life was as she thought it was. Not even Drew. *He claims he sees the dead.* She grasped hold of her suitcase handle tighter with one hand and rubbed the sudden chill bumps off her arm with the other.

When she got to the end of the drive, she walked out onto the deserted road. Dark—except for the light from the moon that shifted and moved as the clouds raced by.

One moment she could see the road ahead of her, the next she was enveloped in inky darkness. She thought she heard Drew calling her name and turned. For a second, she wanted to go back. She wanted to find him and have him assure her that everything would be okay. That this was some crazy dream or misunderstanding. But it wouldn't be okay. Not with him. He said he'd seen her die. Something was seriously screwed up about that.

About him.

Waiting for the cab to come, she walked out onto the Devil's Walk Bridge and looked down into the black waters. Pushing her wind-whipped hair behind her ears, she leaned over the rail and looked into the darkness. Her mother's moonstone pendant hit the wooden railing with a thud.

She grabbed hold of the necklace and stared at it in the dim light. Her mother had left all her belongings behind. She'd taken nothing with her to start her new life. Not even her child.

Laura yanked off the necklace and with the moonstone clutched in her hand drew back her arm. A faint light coming toward her arrested her throw.

But the light came from the murky waters, not the road. As it drew closer, she recognized the old lantern hanging from a long pole.

Laura froze. Terror plunged like ice water through her veins.

The possum hunter.

The light disappeared, and before she could turn or run or scream she saw a flash of bright light, heard a sharp retort. She hit the ground, landing on her back. The air whooshed through her chest. Burning pain stung her shoulder. Her hand came away, wet and sticky.

She looked down and stared in shocked disbelief at the dark stain spreading across her shirt. A small circle that expanded, growing bigger and bigger.

Blood.

Oh my God, I've been shot!

Chapter 18

The sound of a shot echoed through the woods.

"No! Laura!" Delilah turned and ran down the drive.

Drew bolted after her with Jeanne close behind. "Not Laura," he said. *Don't let it be Laura.*

They reached the end of the drive. The only sign of Laura was her suitcase sitting in the deserted road. Headlights shining through the darkness came toward them. They stepped back as a cab pulled to a stop.

"Laura must have called him," Jeanne said, and looked around as if she expected Laura to magically appear out of the trees.

She didn't.

Wind pummeled the trees, forming a cyclone of

leaves and swamp debris that circled around Drew. Rain started to fall. Big heavy drops. Through the beam of the cab's headlights, Drew noticed something lying on the bridge. He ran toward it and saw Delilah's moonstone necklace. He squatted next to it, started to pick it up then stopped. Heart lurching, he pulled back his hand and placed it on his knee.

The pendant was covered in blood.

Cold fear seeped through him. Drew closed his eyes, and reined in his panic.

They had her.

And she was hurt.

A wail sounded from behind him then Delilah was kneeling next to him on the bridge, cradling the necklace in her hands. She opened her palms and stared at the blood smearing her hands and cried even louder.

Another car pulled up next to the cab. Mary jumped out and ran toward them. She didn't say a word, just bent down next to Delilah and held her as she cried.

"She's not dead yet," Drew yelled. "I will find her."

"Drew, wait!" Mary demanded. "You're not ready."

Ignoring her, he turned and headed back up the drive toward his car.

"You must mentally prepare. If you go in there half-cocked and emotional, you'll lose. It won't take much to complete the ritual." Mary ran to catch up to him. She grabbed his arm with her thin hand. The strength of her grip surprised him.

He stopped. Impatience scraped against the fear drumming through him. He didn't have time for this. Not for her, not for anything but finding Laura.

"You must accept who you are, Drew. Embrace your gifts, because that's what they are—gifts. Not a curse. You've pushed away the part of yourself that makes you unique. Special. The part that makes you strong enough to save Laura."

"You mean the spirits?"

"They can help you fight Kafu. They are his victims, too. You need a new plan. Demanding your mother give Laura back won't work."

This wasn't what he wanted to hear. He shook her off and rushed toward the car.

Mary caught up to him, gripping his arm. She dug her fingers into his muscles. Her eyes were bright, intense, as she stared into his. "This is about more than you and your mother. This is about her clan. Her town. Her power. And a very powerful voodoo spirit that will not stop until he gets what he wants. And he wants you, Drew. He has for a very long time. And they're using Laura to get you."

Drew shuddered.

The Great Spirit Kafu talks to me through the water, and after tonight he will talk to you, too. Because we're special, Drew. We've been touched.

As he recalled his mother's fanatical whisperings, despair seeped into his soul as easily as the rain soaked into the ground. "I thought if I could just get Laura to leave, to go back home, she'd be safe. But I couldn't get her to listen."

"She was chosen, Drew. This was her destiny. She took every path the universe offered to get her to this moment. She never veered, not once. It's out of her hands now and it's up to you. Which path will you take?"

"I love her, Mary. I can't let her die. I have to get to the clearing. I have to stop my mother." He opened the driver's door.

"How will you stop her?"

He couldn't answer. He didn't know.

"You've lived your life with your head stuck in the sand. Pull it out and do what has to be done. Stand up for yourself. Take charge or you will become a puppet, a body for a demon."

He stared at the steely determination in her dark Creole eyes and knew she spoke the truth. He had been hiding from his gifts, refusing to face them. "How will this help me or Laura?"

"Open yourself up. Embrace who you are. The spirits have been trying to help you. To guide you. It's time you listened to them."

He ran a hand over his face.

"Part of Kafu came into you from the ritual your mother started on your tenth birthday. It was interrupted. But Kafu gained a foothold. The intensity of your visions, of your ability to see and hear the spirits has been magnified because of that. You learned how to block him and the spirits from talking to you. Once you open yourself back up, you will feel Kafu. You will be able to hear him. He is strong, powerful and seductive. Fight him, push him out."

"You sound insane."

"It is the truth. Let Paul and the other spirits guide you. Push Kafu out. Stop your mother before Laura's blood flows into the swamp. The water is the conduit for Kafu's passage. He will become you, and you him. Once that happens, there will be no going back. Is that clear?"

"Before Laura's blood flows." Drew shuddered thinking of the wound in her shoulder that he'd seen from his vision. Despair threatened once more. He'd spent his whole life fighting the spirits, the voices, and now Mary was asking him to give in. To succumb.

"If I do this, will Laura be saved?"

"I don't know," she whispered. "The cards wouldn't say." She shook her head. "You are almost out of time."

Drew knew once he let the spirits in there would be no going back. Hearing the spirits, constantly seeing them was not something he wanted to live with. If he did this, he'd be opening himself up to a lifetime of harassment. Then, like his mother, he would go insane.

But if he didn't?

He thought of Laura's sweet lips pressed against his and felt his heart lurch. He loved her, and he'd do whatever he could to save her even if it meant going head-to-head with a demon.

Branches slapped against Laura as strong arms carried her through the woods.

"No!" She tried to beat on him, but her right arm was useless. Pain radiated through her shoulder, shooting down her entire right side. Dizziness swept through her.

Raindrops fell, bouncing off her face. They were in complete darkness. Running, each step making her cry out. She bit her tongue and the metallic taste of blood filled her mouth.

The next thing she knew she was in a wooden shack lying on a cot. A candle burning next to her.

Had she blacked out? For how long?

The scruffy face of the hunter stared down at her. Her heart slammed against the wall of her chest.

"You shot me," she croaked. Her mouth parched, her throat scratchy.

"Not me."

Confusion made her head ache.

"Your mother and I have been waiting a long time for this day. We knew it would come and we knew we had to stop it." He grabbed the neck of her shirt and pulled, ripping the fabric.

Laura gasped and cried out.

A hole in her shoulder oozed blood. She stared at it with a detached sense of fascination, knowing that with each drop lost she was moving closer to death. Drew said he saw her die. Was this what he'd seen?

No! It wasn't true.

The hunter shoved white cotton gauze against the wound and applied pressure, pushing painfully down onto her shoulder.

"Stop. Hurts." Tears filled her eyes and streamed down her face.

"Martha needs you to finish what she started. Only with your death can Kafu finish his transformation."

"Not true. Delusional," she muttered, biting down on her lip, trying to stop the pain as he tried to staunch the blood.

"So we waited," he continued unheeded. "And watched."

"You sound like..." She took a shallow breath, then found the strength to say, "My mother."

"She gave up everything for you."

She shook her head. "Threw me away."

Fury blazed through his eyes. He pressed harder on the gauze.

She wailed.

"You are all she thinks about."

"Absurd." She coughed, the pain making her head

swim. She wanted to sleep now. Sleep and let this nightmare be over.

"Evil has had a hold on Martha since the moment she moved into Lionsheart. Why do you think this town has prospered when so many others have failed? And the Larames? Randal went from a small town lawyer to governor and then senator. You think he did that on his good looks alone?" He shook his head. "No. It was Kafu. And what did the spirit want in return?"

She looked away. She didn't want to hear any more.

"Blood."

Her stomach turned. She was going to be sick.

"Blood from my daughter. From you. And too many others over the years to count."

"I need to sit up," she said, and tried to move. "I'm going to be sick."

He shoved a rolled-up blanket under her neck and shoulders, elevating her head. "All so Kafu can walk the earth in the body of her son."

"Drew?" Shock quelled her nausea.

"With Kafu inside him, he'll be able to achieve anything he wants. Anything *she* wants."

Laura shivered as his words penetrated her foggy brain. Not possible. Not real. "Martha loves Drew."

"Yes, and what greater gift can she bestow on her only son than to walk with a god? What do you think 'awakening' means? She's going to awaken the spirit within him."

Laura's eyes shot open. "Will she hurt Drew?"

"Worse. He will be there, but he will be different. The Drew you love will be lost."

Terror seized her.

He held a knife to the candle flame. She tried not to look at it, to think about what he might do with it.

"Help him," she whispered. He brought the knife to the hole in her shoulder and slipped it in. Laura screamed, succumbing to the pain, and slid into the darkness.

"All right," Drew whispered and took a deep breath. "Tell me what to do."

"Good." Mary nodded in satisfaction. "Close your eyes. Take three deep cleansing breaths. Pull in the white light and exhale out your fear and negative energy like a black toxic cloud. Do you see it?"

"Yes."

"Good. As you pull in the white light, let it fill you with warmth. Know it is here to help you. Welcome it in. Embrace it. Paul is that light. The other spirits are part of that light. Open yourself up, Drew. Let them in."

He did as she asked, inhaling the white light, exhaling his fears. Focusing, concentrating. He remembered Laura as he'd made love to her, expanding then shattering into a million bright lights. Was he seeing a vision of her after tonight? After his mother killed her?

Pushing away his despair, he again exhaled the black cloud of negativity and fear and drew in the light. He could do this. He could save Laura.

When he opened his eyes, he saw the white light surrounding Paul, and suddenly he could hear his voice. As clearly as he had when Paul was alive.

"Be strong, Drew. We can fight him. Together."

A wave of dizziness crashed over him. Drew faltered. Mary grabbed onto him, steadying him. He saw the lights of the spirits surrounding him. There were so many. All Kafu's victims?

He shuddered.

Something expanded within him. Growing.

"Breathe in the light, Drew. Feel it. Absorb it. Picture the brick-and-mortar walls you've erected in your mind then knock them down. Let the light in. Let it fill you."

He did as she said. A fierce wave of noise hit him. He smashed his hands against his ears, trying to block out the otherworldly chatter.

"Tune it out, Drew. Focus on one voice at a time. You have the control. The power. Visualize what you want."

Her words barely reached through the din. He followed what she said, and found the relief he needed to be able to be able to function.

Paul stood in front of him. "Fight him, Drew. Don't let him in. Don't let him have my daughter."

Drew felt the presence inside him expanding. Filling him. Something big. Something powerful. Something a lot stronger than he was.

Kafu.

The door to the shack burst open with a thunderous roar. The walls shook. The hunter jumped up so fast his chair fell over. The blurred figures of two men filled the room. Laura blinked, trying to clear her vision.

Hands grabbed her, pulling. White-hot pain burned through her shoulder.

She screamed.

"Fight them, Laura. Don't give in," the hunter yelled. "Do it for your mother."

One of the men hit him. Hard. He crumpled to the floor, looking at her with eyes full of despair, before they rolled back and closed.

"Charlie?" Was he dead? Had they killed him?

Fear flooded through her. Rough hands yanked her up off the cot and through the door. She screamed and choked. The pain in her shoulder was excruciating as they forced her through the woods. Blackness edged her vision, threatening to pull her down. She couldn't succumb. She had to fight it.

She had to live!

She barely noticed the rain had stopped as they

dragged her to a car parked in the road. One man opened the car's back door, another pushed her inside. They climbed in the front and put the car in gear. Gravel flew as the car sped down the road.

Branches scraped metal. Tires spun as they took a corner too fast and pulled into a clearing. They were barely stopped when people gathered around the car and opened the door.

"Take her to the water," a woman yelled in a high-pitched excited voice.

Hands pulled her out, half dragging and half carrying her toward a bonfire lit at the water's edge. A crowd of people gathered around them. Why were there so many? Why wasn't anyone helping her?

Cold fingers smeared her head with oil as they walked. Voices chanted weird words that sounded terrifyingly familiar. Firelight flickered, black smoke filled the air...and then she remembered. She remembered everything.

Shock trembled through her. It was true. All of it. Her mother, Jeanne and Charlie the crazy hunter, they had all tried to tell her. Tried to stop her. But she had refused to listen. To believe.

Everything they had said was true.

Wide-eyed, she looked around her. A raging fire roared.

Candles burned. Animals screamed. People prowled about as they dragged her to the water's edge.

To Martha.

Only Martha looked taller. Bigger. Wavy blue lines covered her cheeks. Her hair was piled high on her head, the long column of her neck bare.

How could Laura have not seen or believed what everyone had been trying to tell her? Tears filled her eyes. Now it was too late. For her. For her mother. For Drew.

Fight, Laura. The hunter's words rang through her mind.

But how?

Suddenly Drew walked into the clearing. She almost called out to him, but stopped herself. He looked different. Colder. More distant. His eyes grazed over her, but didn't linger.

Fear twisted inside her gut. Something had gone wrong. Something had happened to him.

He will be there, but he will be different.

Chapter 19

Drew walked into the clearing as if he belonged there. Because he did. All this—the candles, the altars, the animal sacrifices—they were for him.

"Focus on the light, Drew," Mary said, touching his arm. He brushed her off and kept walking.

People stood back as he continued forward, heads bowed, lips moving in feverish mutterings. Shadows flitted among them. Some dark. Some light. The dead. The *powerless.*

He saw Laura being dragged toward the water. Blood seeped from a wound in her shoulder. Blood spilled for him.

Blood that would make his journey complete.

He walked toward his mother. She smiled, knowing

he'd changed, knowing he'd let the spirits in. That he'd opened himself up to the presence that was in him. To Kafu.

Her eyes flicked to Paul, who traveled beside him, but his presence had no effect on her or on what was about to happen. Paul was nothing but a shadow, trapped like a flitting moth between here and there.

Drew's mother took his hand and led him to the high-back chair. He sat in the enclosure and let a tall black man paint his face and whisper the sacred words about honor and homage.

As the man worked, his mother took a rooster out of a cage and laid the squirming bird on a large butcher-block table. She picked up a meat cleaver and with one vicious whack, chopped off its head.

With a hallowed gesture, she lifted the carcass up over her head, then grabbed its feet and swung it back and forth. Splattering blood, chanting as she walked, forming a trail all the way to the water's edge.

To Laura.

He saw her standing there, the light surrounding her body brighter than most. He was intrigued by her light. He wanted to touch her, to feel her light within him.

You can have her. You can have it all.

He stood and walked toward her. Toward the water. Yes, he would have it all.

* * *

Horrified, Laura watched Martha approach her, the dead rooster dangling from her hand, swinging back and forth, the poor bird's blood flying everywhere.

Then Drew stepped forward. In the glow of the bonfire's light, he stared at her with cold eyes. No affection. No humanity. No Drew. He was alien to her and it chilled her to the bone.

The two men holding her arms pulled her out into the swamp. She twisted in their grasp, the pain in her shoulder cutting through her, almost making her collapse. A wave of dizziness fell over her and they dragged her farther into the water. They stopped and pushed her onto her knees.

"Martha, please!" she begged as the woman walked toward her.

Stopping in front of her, Martha swung the rooster. Blood dropped onto Laura's head and trickled down her cheeks. Her stomach heaved. She gagged and leaned forward. The men jerked her upright, pulling at her shoulder. She cried out, bringing a gleam of triumph to Martha's cold eyes.

Laura gasped for breath as sobs overtook her. She was going to die. And Drew was going to stand there and watch...*the sacrifice.*

Martha dropped the rooster's carcass into the swamp. She reached into her satchel and Laura's heart froze. Martha raised her hand high above her head, a long, wickedly sharp knife clutched in her fist.

"Drew!" Laura screamed.

Drew stepped forward. Her frantic gaze swung to his. For a second, something flickered in his eyes—pain? Fear?

"Drew, help me!"

"Mother, stop!" Drew yelled, moving toward them.

A chant rose up from the people on the shoreline. A shout came from the clearing. Laura saw her mother running toward her, yelling and waving her arms.

"Delilah." An odd smile lifted Martha's lips, stopping Laura's heart cold.

"Oh, my God. Mom!" Laura struggled against the men holding her, oblivious to the pain.

Her mother reached the water and plowed in toward them. The two men holding Laura jerked her upright, and squeezed her arms tighter.

In a graceful arc, Martha swung back her arm and threw the knife. It hit her mother, embedding itself deep in her chest.

Laura let out an ear-piercing wail as her mother fell forward. Drew rushed forward and caught her. Holding her, he looked down at her in shocked disbelief. But as her blood spread into his shirt, and dripped into the water, something happened to him. He changed. His face hardened, his eyes grew cold.

Suddenly he was holding her as if she were nothing.

"Drew, help her," Laura cried.

But she could tell by the glazed look in his eyes, by the lack of focus and emotion that there would be no help from him.

Not for her and not for her mother, who had just run to her death trying to save her.

Anguish sucked away whatever fight Laura had left in her. Charlie had been right. Her mother had loved her.

Only now it was too late. For her. For Drew.

For all of them.

As Drew held Delilah's body in his arms, he felt her blood flow across his hands, warm and sticky, and drip into the water. And with each drop, the presence grew within him. The power consumed everything as it filled him. Fear, pain, loss, doubt—it all disappeared, making him feel stronger, better.

And he wanted to feel better. He craved the power surging through him. But he knew if he succumbed, he'd be lost. And Laura would die.

He fought the pressure building, expanding within him. Suddenly, people looked different. The woman bleeding in his arms was a power source. Something that would feed him. With each drop he grew bigger, stronger. Invincible.

And he liked it.

No! This was Miss Delilah bleeding in his arms. *Fight him!*

His mother walked toward him and placed her

hands on top of Delilah's body. "Let her go, Drew. Let her death feed you."

Delilah looked up at him, her blue eyes wide and pleading. He could see the energy of her light force dimming as the blood flowed out of her body and into the water.

"Drew, help her!" Laura begged. The despair in her voice touched something deep within him. Something that wanted to listen, wanted to help. That something moved within him, pulling at him, fighting the surging power building inside him.

He stepped backward, carrying Delilah toward shore.

"Drop her," his mother demanded. She rushed forward, pushing down on Delilah.

They struggled, and Delilah sank lower into the water, beneath the dark surface. Power surged through him, warm, heady and intoxicating.

Laura screamed.

The pressure within him clawed to the surface.

"No!" A shout came from the trees. The blast of a gun.

His mother stiffened. Her back arched, her eyes widened. Blood seeped from her heart through her red robes.

"Drew," she whispered, and collapsed into the water.

Somewhere deep inside him, he heard a howl of pain.

* * *

Laura wrenched free from her shocked captors and stumbled to where her mother had fallen. She plunged her arms beneath the water and lifted her mother up. Pain constricted her shoulder, making it difficult to breathe as she struggled to pull her mother to shore.

"Drew!"

He turned to her, looking lost and confused.

"Help me!"

He shook his head clear and took her mother out of her arms then carried her toward shore. Her mother coughed, choking up swamp water. Charlie ran toward them, a rifle in his hand. He dropped to the ground next to them.

A loud siren wailed and flashing lights from a sheriff's car and an ambulance cut through the darkness under the trees.

The dazed crowd scattered, running into the woods.

"Drew, are you okay?" Laura asked, concerned by the lack of emotion on his face or warmth in his eyes.

Laura felt a hand on her arm and turned to find a paramedic standing beside her. "You're bleeding. We have to get you looked at. What about him?" He gestured toward Drew.

"I don't know. He must be in shock," she said, and hoped that was what was wrong with him.

The paramedic led her to the ambulance and helped her up inside with her mother.

Her mother was conscious. Tears swam in her eyes as she reached for Laura's hand.

"Are you okay?" Laura asked, and knew by the pallor of her skin that she wasn't. Her heart plummeted. "I'm so sorry I didn't listen to you. I was just so hurt, so mad."

Her mother squeezed her hand. "You never stopped fighting," she whispered. "Proud of you."

Laura's throat closed and shooting pinpricks moved across the bridge of her nose as she fought back her tears.

"Love you." Her mother's eyes closed as she drifted to sleep.

Only two little words, yet Laura felt them deep within her. Losing the battle, tears spilled down her face as her heart expanded with bittersweet joy.

As the ambulance pulled away, she saw Drew standing in the clearing, standing apart from everyone else, looking out at the water.

He will be there, but he will be different. The Drew you love will be lost.

Chapter 20

A short while after checking out of the hospital, Laura pulled the rental car up in front of Lionsheart. It had been a long night, but it looked as though her mom would make it. She only hoped she could say the same for Drew.

Staring up at the old house, she believed now that spirits and evil did exist and they thrived in places like Lionsheart.

She hurried toward the front door, once again filled with fear mingled with hope. Once again determined to find what she came for. Family. *Love.*

And yet as she stood on the front porch, she hesitated, afraid what she'd find when she opened the door. Afraid of what Drew might have become.

She took a deep breath and slowly opened the door. She crept into the house. Candles were burning in every room. Not regular candles, but Martha's vinegar-scented ceremonial candles.

To complete the ritual?

She was supposed to die. That meant, once again, the ritual wasn't completed.

You can't go anywhere near Drew. Do you understand that? Kafu still needs your sacrifice to make the transition complete.

Jeanne's warning earlier at the hospital rang through her mind. With it came the fear, making her numb. She couldn't turn her back on Drew, not if there was the slightest chance of saving him. No matter what the risk. She couldn't leave him. She took a deep breath and forced her feet to move.

Drew was sitting in the living room staring up at her mother's portrait. "I knew you would come," he said.

A chill snaked down her spine. "Did you?"

"Yes. *He* said you would."

"He?"

"Drew." He looked up at her and his cold vacant stare froze the blood in her veins.

"Drew was right," she said. "I came because I love him. And if you're a part of him, I love you, too." She forced her legs to move toward him.

"You're surrounded by light, you know. It's everywhere. It's intoxicating." He sniffed the air, as if he could smell her. As if he were breathing her in.

She shuddered.

He stood as she approached him. She placed a hand on his chest. He sucked in a breath and, for a second, something flashed in his eyes. A glimmer, a shadow of Drew?

She grasped onto that flicker of him and leaned forward pressing her lips to his. They were stiff and cold, but she didn't care because she knew Drew was inside there. She knew he could hear her.

If she could just make him feel her love then perhaps she could get him to come back to her.

She deepened the kiss, ignoring how different he felt and started unbuttoning her shirt. They had a special connection when they touched each other, when they made love. She'd never felt that strong, binding connection with anyone else, and somehow she knew, it was the one way to reach him. To pull him back to her.

She stripped down until she stood naked in front of him. "Drew, come back to me. Feel my touch, my love. Focus on me."

He put his hands on her shoulders, lightly caressing her skin and, for a second, his touch felt like Drew's, his lips moved like Drew's. She smiled and unclasped his pants then pulled him down onto the floor with her. She kissed him again, deeper, even as she felt his hands slip around her neck.

* * *

"Drew!" Paul's voice boomed through Drew's mind. "Hurry!"

Drew wanted to hurry. He knew he had to hurry, but he couldn't remember why. Everything was so dark, except for a pinprick of light off in the distance. He moved toward it and, as he got closer, he heard Laura's voice, he felt her sweet touch. He must be dreaming.

Love and tenderness overwhelmed him.

Then he saw her beneath him. Felt himself moving inside her. Saw hands wrapped around her neck. Her blue eyes bulging, her beautiful lips parted, gasping for air.

No!

Drew jerked back, pulling his hands from Laura's neck.

She gasped a breath.

The presence within him howled and struggled to push him back down into the darkness. Drew fought with everything he had. Laura's light was strong. He flung himself toward it. He started to move within it, faster, harder. He felt it enveloping him. He felt her everywhere, her breath on his neck, her tears on his skin. Her warmth surrounding him.

Her strength filled him. He pushed against the presence, visualizing it as a black toxic cloud. The more he pushed, the stronger he became.

"Drew!" Laura screamed, and thrust against

him. She burst into a million bright tiny lights. They circled around him. He breathed them in, breathed her in and pushed the darkness out. The foul dark cloud of evil.

Deep inside him, he heard a roar of protest. The presence surged within him. A tension expanding, growing so big he thought he would explode from the inside out.

He fell on his back and it burst out of him, a black lethal cloud that reached for the sky.

"Oh my God, Drew. Drew!" Laura shook him hard.

He opened his eyes and stared at her and thought she had to be the most beautiful woman he has ever seen.

"Hi," he said, and smiled.

She stared intently at him for a moment then grinned.

"What?"

"You're giving me that crooked smile again."

"My smile is not crooked."

"Yes, it is."

He reached up and touched her hair and let the overwhelming love he felt for her fill him. He looked around the room and remembered where he was, and everything that had happened.

"You shouldn't have come here," he said.

"I couldn't leave you. I love you. And I refuse to let you go."

He wrapped his arms tightly around her waist and pulled her next to him. "Good. Because I love you, and I have no intention of letting you out of my sight. Ever again. What do you say we get out of here?"

"Where to?"

"I was thinking the desert."

"Really?" she asked, pulling on her clothes.

"As long as we're together, I'll go anywhere with you."

Hand in hand they walked out of the house and as they approached the car, Drew turned back. A flicker, a shadow that, for a second, looked like Paul stood in the window. A blue-green light flashed, then it was gone.

Was this what it would be like? Without Kafu's presence within him, were flickers and shadows of the dead all he would see? The thought filled him with giddy relief.

Suddenly flames devoured the curtains behind the windows.

Drew stopped. "The house is on fire."

Laura looked back at the house, then at him and smiled. "Let it burn. The earth around here needs a good cleansing."

They got into the car and drove away and though Drew couldn't tell if Paul was there or not, he lifted his hand in a gesture of thanks and said a silent goodbye.

* * * * *

nocturne™

COMING NEXT MONTH

Available September 28, 2010

#97 THE KEEPERS
The Keepers
Heather Graham

#98 POISONED KISSES
Stephanie Draven

HNCNM0910

HARLEQUIN®
A Romance
FOR EVERY MOOD™

See below for a sneak peek at
our inspirational line, Love Inspired®.
Introducing HIS HOLIDAY BRIDE
by bestselling author Jillian Hart

Autumn Granger gave her horse rein to slide toward the town's new sheriff.

"Hey, there." The man in a brand-new Stetson, black T-shirt, jeans and riding boots held up a hand in greeting. He stepped away from his four-wheel drive with "Sheriff" in black on the doors and waded through the grasses. "I'm new around here."

"I'm Autumn Granger."

"Nice to meet you, Miss Granger. I'm Ford Sherman, from Chicago." He knuckled back his hat, revealing the most handsome face she'd ever seen. Big blue eyes contrasted with his sun-tanned complexion.

"I'm guessing you haven't seen much open land. Out here, you've got to keep an eye on cows or they're going to tear your vehicle apart."

"What?" He whipped around. Sure enough, mammoth black-and-white creatures had started to gnaw on his four-wheel drive. They clustered like a mob, mouths and tongues and teeth bent on destruction. One cow tried to pry the wiper off the windshield, another chewed on the side mirror. Several leaned through the open window, licking the seats.

"Move along, little dogie." He didn't know the first thing about cattle.

The entire herd swiveled their heads to study him curiously. Not a single hoof shifted. The animals soon returned to chewing, licking, digging through his possessions.

Autumn laughed, a warm and wonderful sound. "Thanks,

I needed that." She then pulled a bag from behind her saddle and waved it at the cows. "Look what I have, guys. Cookies."

Cows swung in her direction, and dozens of liquid brown eyes brightened with cookie hopes. As she circled the car, the cattle bounded after her. The earth shook with the force of their powerful hooves.

"Next time, you're on your own, city boy." She tipped her hat. The cowgirl stayed on his mind, the sweetest thing he had ever seen.

Will Ford be able to stick it out in the country
to find out more about Autumn?
Find out in HIS HOLIDAY BRIDE
by bestselling author Jillian Hart,
available in October 2010
only from Love Inspired®.

SHLIEXP1010